November

November

Fragments in a Nondescript Style

Gustave Flaubert

Translated by Andrew Brown

ET REMOTISSIMA PROPE

Hesperus Classics

Hesperus Classics
Published by Hesperus Press Limited
4 Rickett Street, London sw6 1ru
www.hesperuspress.com

November first published in French as *Novembre* in *Oeuvres de jeunesse* in 1910
This translation first published by Hesperus Press Limited, 2005

Foreword © Nadine Gordimer, 2005
Introduction and English language translation © Andrew Brown, 2005

Designed and typeset by Fraser Muggeridge
Printed in Jordan by Jordan National Press

ISBN: 1-84391-112-4

CONTENTS

November. 'When the trees have lost their leaves, when the sky at sunset still preserves the russet hue that fills with gold the withered grass, it is sweet to watch the final fading of the fires that until recently burnt within you.'

Autumn. And it is with a man's recall of that season of life that there begins the most beautiful, unsparing, shaming and unashamed, emotionally and morally pitiless evocation of its antithesis, the season of fires ignited. Flaubert's novella is an unsurpassed testament of adolescence.

Gustave Flaubert was barely twenty years old when he completed it in 1842. He was the one burning. 'The heart enters puberty before the body.' As a schoolboy aged fifteen he fell worshipfully in love with somebody's wife. On his first travels beyond Rouen, where he was born, and still a virgin at eighteen despite tortuous sexual desires, he was made love to by the daughter of the proprietor of the hotel where he lodged in Marseilles. He did not forget either conquest the women made of him, soul or body; they were transposed into one, the woman Marie, in this book.

This I learn from reading the many biographies of the author. Flaubert, more than any other fiction writer I can cite, including Marcel Proust, has been subjected to the process of taking the writer's creation as a kind of documentary basis for what is more interesting to explore: his / her life. It's not what you write, it's who you are. This guesswork on the processes of the imagination is surely a denigration – if one made unconsciously by scholars – of literature: the act of creation itself. Fiction cannot be 'explained' by autobiography; it remains, like the composition of music, a profound mystery, while a source of human understanding only the arts can offer.

I give the hotel keeper's daughter simply as an example of the still fashionable literary methodology – not outdated along with the psychological novel but somehow reinforced by postmodern theory that anything pertinent to the author, even childhood snaps reproduced in the text, belongs in his / her fiction. I don't care – and, frankly, I think Flaubert's reader won't care – whether or not the transporting experience of this book is really that of the author's young life. All that counts is that it is a work of genius written by a twenty year old. Genius: as always, on that extremely rare level of mind and spirit, the exploration of human motivation, action and feeling remains relevant, becomes again and again astonishingly contemporary in generations long after that within which it was conceived.

The years on which the narrator looks back from his November were the reign of King Louis Philippe, 1830 48, years of post-Napoleonic disillusion, when revolutionary change as an agent to bring about justice, end privilege and corruption, create values to replace those shabbily glittering, seemed impossible. There was nothing to believe in, secular or religious, that was not a sham in relation to deep needs. Nothing to aspire to beyond materialism; and if resigned to this, no youth had the chance of access without sponsorship in high places. There are many countries in our twenty-first century where young people today experience the same frustration, malaise, updating the nineteenth-century escape to absinthe and opium by whatever alcoholic concoction at hand, and various narcotic means.

Flaubert's reluctant law student, from a provincial bourgeois family with unrealised Voltairean ideas, has no name as narrator, drawing one without intermediary breath-to-breath into his life. He dispenses with his study assignments summarily in favour of poetry, unlikely ambitions in the arts, and fantasies: 'I would follow my thoughts as far as they would take me, I would examine them from every angle, I would plumb their depths... I would build my own palaces and take up residence in them like an emperor, I would dig out the diamonds from every mine and strew them in bucketfuls on the path along which I was to travel.'

The awakening of the imagination comes through the evocative power of words, and so does the sexual awakening. 'Certain words overwhelmed me, *woman* and *mistress* in particular... and the magic of the mere name' threw the adolescent 'into prolonged raptures'. This is the genesis of an erotic narrative, an achievement that has nothing to do with pornography and everything to do with acknowledgement of the sexual drive in symbiosis with the spirit and intellect.

The 'mystery of woman' obsesses him in the streets with small details enchantingly described, from which he creates for himself the whole woman, tries to attach to each passing foot 'a body, each body to an idea, and all these movements to their different goals; I wondered where all these steps were heading.' His desires being unsatisfied, he revenges himself by rejecting what has denied their satisfaction. He's taken pleasure in watching prostitutes and seeing rich beauties in their carriages, but this turns to savage disgust – for them all – and extends to both levels of society they represent. The rebel without a cause, an empty heart, wants to lose himself in crowds. 'What, then, is this nagging disquiet? We are as proud of it as we are proud of our genius, and we conceal it like some secret love.' (We'd diagnose depression, today.) His desperate plunges into communion with nature are no consolation; forces as erotic as sexual fantasies are what he enjoys there, only reinforcing his sexual frustration.

'Only some great love might have rescued me from my plight.'

Unable to act, suffocated by youthful arrogance and fantasy, the young man not only has not realised the love – sexual and ideal – he places at the centre of being; he still looks for the sign that will beckon him to it. Seeking distraction, he responds to a sign that would seem to have no relation to this depth of need; he accepts the invitation in the eyes of a prostitute. If he has no name of his own he cares to give the reader, she has called herself Marie. Relieved of his virginity with a voluptuousness beyond the conceptions of his fantasies, he goes home with self-repulsion and returns with renewed desire. What could be described too inadequately as an affair begins. She is older than him, in every way, years and breadth of experiences; a beauty in whom we recognise some of the characteristics of the unapproachable women he has idealised. The complexity of what we glibly term sexual satisfaction is conveyed subtly, marvellously, as something that truly can be *read*. Hyperbole has to be revaluated, in this prose. The professionally uncalled-for passion that has come about between her and this young initiate bonds the paradox of the situation into a communion of melancholy and sensuality. Love?

He has not known love. She has been used by many men but not known love; both despair of ever knowing it – yet, while doubting its existence within the morals and mores of their time, continue tortuously to seek it. From her, the woman who belongs to every man, he hears the 'first words of love I had ever heard in my life'. With her body lying upon him in exquisitely described awareness of her physicality, he is led to receive her in her whole being, not a means, a substitute for the unattainable. 'Seeing this woman, so melancholy in pleasure… I guessed at the countless terrible passions that must have left their furrows on her like a thunderbolt, to judge from the remaining traces; what a pleasure it would have been to hear her relate her life to me, as I was seeking all that was resounding and vibrant in human existence, the world of great passions and lovely tears.' He begs her for her story. Marie is aware that a prostitute's life outside the bed is not a story clients want to be reminded of. But as often throughout this book the flow of intimacy, irony, contemplation and self-scrutiny is suddenly stoppered: there's a curt statement that switches your mind to a new possibility of revelation:

'Yes, I can tell it to you.'

And in these words there's unspoken nuance on the strange nature of their closeness. Why 'to him'?

She begins a soliloquy that could be lifted out of the book as a novella in itself. Flaubert complained in his early writings that language is inadequate to depths of feeling. This is overwhelmingly disproved by himself in Marie's telling of her story. One might doubt whether a woman of her brutally humble background could have such a command of words to embody feelings? What can't be questioned – only received with amazement – is how a male writer could enter identity with a woman out of his class and kind so utterly. This is the writer's clairvoyance, that all writers share to a certain extent, which this time is beyond what inevitably comes to mind in comparison – James Joyce's creation of the inner musings of Molly Bloom. The twenty-year-old Flaubert achieved close to the great Hungarian writer-critic, Georg Lukács's definition of the fiction writer's unachievable ultimate aim: wholeness; how to express *all*. Flaubert's narrator says he is 'like a bee gathering my nourishment and sustenance from everything I encountered'. Flaubert, creating him and the woman Marie, attains this – for *his work*. The brief novel, with its hurtingly fresh evocation of passion for nature and sexual love as two fused expressions of the same primal source, its implicit social critique, linking individuals to their time, is shocking, yes – not in the sense of offensive, rather in the sense of awakening you as you read to areas of thought evaded, hidden. I leave it to you, the reader, to reach The End – at what point the author puts aside his account of his narrator's life, and turns away to begin the novels of his celebrated maturity, including *Madame Bovary*.

Gustave Flaubert's famously cryptic remark of that period: '*Madame Bovary, c'est moi.*' Madame Bovary is myself. In this early novel: all the manifestations of life revealed are somewhere buried in all of us. We were or are young. *C'est nous.* It's us.

– *Nadine Gordimer, 2005*

INTRODUCTION

Towards the end of *Manhattan,* the hapless, indecisive Woody Allen character, Isaac, is lying on the couch in his apartment talking into a tape recorder in a bout of self-analysis as he tries to find some meaning in his unsatisfying existence. What is it that makes life worth living? With many 'ums' and 'ahs', he comes up with a list: Groucho Marx, baseball player Willie Mays, the second movement of the 'Jupiter' symphony, Louis Armstrong's recording of 'Potato Head Blues', Swedish movies (by Ingmar Bergman, presumably), Marlon Brando, Frank Sinatra, 'those incredible apples and pears by Cézanne', the crabs at Sam Wo's. This list has become canonical; it is regularly trotted out as one of the great screen quotations, perhaps since the delights it catalogues chime in so well with the cultural proclivities of Allen's target audience, who can all identify with (even if they do not share) his tastes – a nice mixture of 'high' culture (Mozart and Cézanne) and 'popular culture' (Armstrong and Sinatra), of comedy and sport, food and art. But not even these cultural riches seem able to overcome the note of loss and rancour pervading *Manhattan* (one of whose themes, after all, is the bickering and neurosis, the ego trips and anxieties inseparable from cultural life): at the end, Gershwin's *Rhapsody in Blue* sings out in elegiac distress over those beautiful but oddly bleak skyscrapers.

There are certain analogies between the world of Woody Allen and that of Flaubert, and they are made clear in a particularly succinct way in *November*. Flaubert's narrator is dreamy and indecisive, like so many of Allen's schleppers and schlemiels, overburdened with introspection and just as unable to find an ostensible reason for living. Flaubert's unnamed protagonist (let us call him the Narrator, in anticipation of his quasi-anonymous and even more radically indeterminate avatars in the modernist fictions of Proust and Beckett) is not going through a midlife crisis as is Allen's Isaac, but he is afflicted by its youthful equivalent, puberty. He is a young man with all the advantages attendant on being born into the bourgeoisie; he is, in addition, intelligent, imaginative, un-trammelled; he has everything to live for. And that is one of the problems: *everything*. Every possibility lies open to him; no social obligations weigh him down; the world lies all before him, where to choose... He is (as was the young Flaubert) gently eased into studying law, like so many other young Frenchmen of his generation, but is quite without vocation or ambition (why study law when there are so many other things he could equally well do?); he refuses to adopt any determinate personality because this would mean limiting himself and betraying the countless *other* opportunities the world offers him. These opportunities do not free him, but paralyse him. When there are so many possibilities for experience and travel, why choose to do, or be, *this* rather than *that*? Why fall for *this* woman rather than *that* one? Any finite choice is bound to be arbitrary and derisory in the face of the infinitude of life that will always ironically transcend it. This is the dilemma of a certain romanticism: it tries to keep faith with the infinite by refusing to endorse the definitive value of anything finite, in case the latter becomes an idol. This attitude may be mistaken (in that it fails to see how the finite and the infinite are dynamically interrelated, so that faith with the infinite may best be kept by those who focus strenuously on what is defined and limited), but it is what gives many of Flaubert's protagonists (from the Narrator of *November* to Emma Bovary, or the Frédéric of *Sentimental Education*), their divine – or all-too-human – discontent.

Flaubert's Narrator has his moments of enjoyment: sitting round the stove on a cold winter's day chatting with his school chums, or walking ecstatically by the sea. But he would probably not come up with a list of the good things in life, like Isaac's, with its pleasingly fetishistic character (Isaac lives in a world that is so much more orientated to cultural commodification); what makes life worth living for Flaubert's Narrator is, rather, something much less particular – an occasional but intensely epiphanic sense of pantheistic absorption in the world as a whole, rather than the connoisseur's delight in any one manifestation of it. But in both Allen and Flaubert, there is something that at least provisionally goes beyond this panoramic survey of the Garden of Earthly Delights, whether it is couched in Isaac's list of desiderata, or in the Narrator's sense of fusion with all creation. At the end of his litany of the things that save life from meaninglessness, Isaac pauses, and then adds: 'Uh... Tracy's face.' Whereupon he rises from his couch and runs through the grainy, black-and-white streets of bustling, indifferent New York to see Tracy – but too late, as she is just about to set off to London for six months, no doubt never to return (at least, not as the Tracy he loves, though the film leaves the question open). And in *November*, the Narrator's sudden passion for Marie, which begins as lust for the one woman who happens to be available and starts to metamorphose into something slightly closer to the obsessive and particular possessiveness of love, also seems to offer a transcendence of the catalogue, only for this hope too to be dashed by her disappearance. A loved person is never just yet another item, thing or object in the world, but a subject, a world in itself: Tracy's face, for Isaac, and Marie for the Narrator. With Tracy and Marie, 'I like' (as in liking Mozart and Sinatra and Sam Wo's) becomes 'I love'.

This love is, in *November*, not only short-lived but one-dimensional. *Memoirs of a Madman* had given us sacred love – modelled on the teenage Flaubert's platonic and idealising love for Elisa Foucault (there fictionalised as Maria). *November* gives us its profane counterpart, also based on Flaubert's own life – this time his first intense sexual experience, a brief holiday romance in Marseilles with Eulalie Foucaud de Langlade. (There is a nice similarity between the names, Elisa Foucault and Eulalie Foucaud, projected into the near-equivalence of their fictional counterparts Maria in the *Memoirs* and Marie in *November*, as if sacred and profane loves could be melded together by fiat.) It seems that Eulalie, older and more experienced, took the initiative; it is certain that one of the things analysed most probingly (and effectively) in *November* is masculine passivity. (And Sartre in turn devotes countless pages in his vast study of Flaubert, *The Family Idiot*, to Gustave's own, very un-Sartrean, passivity.) The Narrator, before his encounter with Marie, wanders round the streets and country lanes dreaming as much of 'being possessed' as of 'possessing'; indeed, those quaint words seem even more inadequate than usual, as his pantheistic reveries are based on a longing for a kind of osmotic fusion in which the usual tiresome sexual roles, 'active' and 'passive', can be safely ignored. It is no surprise to learn from his correspondence that the young Flaubert fantasised (in an overtly playful rather than anguished way, but intensely nonetheless) about self-castration, and dreamt (as does his Narrator) of becoming a woman. In *November*, the encounter with Marie leads to a sexual chiasmus: she seems the more masculine character, he the more feminine; she is active (almost predatory: she has become a prostitute because she likes sex, not – as is more usual – out of dire economic necessity), he is passive. He has a series of situations and moods; she has a story to tell, and despite the unlikely eloquence the text attributes to her, it is a strangely haunting one – more than just a premonition of Emma Bovary's longings. The Narrator thus identifies Marie (rather glibly) as a soul sister: they meet at the crossroads of gender, as it were, and are both longing for something that sexuality at first seems to offer, but actually withholds. Sexuality, the secular form of transcendence, leads to a bad infinity ('more! more!') – and thus ultimately fails to escape from the catalogue of things. She will always be looking for a real lover; he will search fruitlessly for an object (or activity) that will live up to his ideal. In their respective quests, they will exhaust the world's resources, and for each other they will become merely rungs on a never-ending ladder to nowhere. No doubt Tracy, too, will become just one more of Isaac's women, one more 'love'. Perhaps neither the Maria of *Memoirs of a Madman* (the permanent, paralysing spiritual ideal, perched conveniently on a pedestal) nor the Marie of *November* (the all-too-available flesh) is really loved by their respective narrators (at least not in the unromantic sense that the latter actually have to live with them – always the supreme trial), and the dichotomy of Madonna and whore, although explored with great lucidity by Flaubert, is never resolved. It appears that Flaubert, who for all his perfectionism remained fond of this unpublished youthful piece, once promised to read *November* to Baudelaire – who would have recognised this last topos with grim satisfaction.

November is already exploring one of its author's most constant preoccupations – his sense that language gives us intelligibility but sacrifices the particular to do so. Flaubert, a literary prodigy who encountered life first through imagining it and writing about it, was prone to the nominalist temptation of thinking that, merely by labelling the items in the world (things in general), you can know it (in its particulars). The Narrator of *November* likewise is very good at identifying the *sorts* of things in the world – he has read about them and spends hours re-imagining them. He knows the words 'woman', 'mistress', 'adultery' before becoming personally acquainted with their referents. Words will open up his desire, but simultaneously make its satisfaction impossible. (Emma Bovary likewise dreams of finding a perfect instantiation of the words 'happiness', 'passion' and 'intoxication' – words that had seemed so alluring in books – and when she thinks she has found it, in Rodolphe, she is all too happy to identify this most intensely personal token with its type: having at last committed adultery she exults to herself, 'I have a lover! A lover!', i.e. 'I am *the sort of woman* that has a lover!') Language, which makes the world knowable, thereby, at least for Flaubert's characters, makes any real experience of it secondary and belated. This, again, may well be a mistaken and simplistic view of language, but it gives Flaubert's world its characteristic pathos. In that world, life is always struggling against its own clichés, and any apparent originality is soon revealed as a copy – just as the Narrator's desire is at first, before its momentary crystallisation in the shape of Marie, a desire for desire. He dreams (as she does) of the Orient, that place of exotic otherness par excellence, but what he peoples it with are *sorts* of things, stock situations, brightly coloured vignettes (what Rimbaud would ironically call 'Illuminations') – a melding of the stereotypes that can be picked and mixed from the sweet-shop of cultural references. At one moment, the Narrator calls a camel 'the ship of the desert': years later, in the *Dictionary of Received Ideas* that Flaubert probably intended to append to his last work, *Bouvard and*

Pécuchet, we find (inevitably) 'the camel is the ship of the desert' as an example of the mindless clichés that kept polite nineteenth-century conversation going. Already in *November*, it seems as if familiarity with the world conceals it from us. The Narrator realises this with great lucidity. His identity is not essentially predicated (as is that of Isaac in Manhattan) on liking certain specific things: he is too vague for that, his personality as yet (and perhaps permanently) too indeterminate. He is the modern subject as undefined possibility, pure velleity: he would (in his imagination) like to be (or to have been) many things (an emperor, an eagle, a tyrant, an Indian perishing beneath the juggernaut, a woman, an African explorer, a starveling). Like Keats's artist figure, he has negative capability – but he never converts that negativity into something more substantial by actually becoming an artist. Like many an adolescent male engorged by sexual desire, he suffers from an Ixion complex, seeking to embrace the clouds (Ixion lay with a cloud shaped like Hera, thinking that he was enjoying the favours of the goddess herself): but he carries that complex over into all desire, which, even when it is apparently satisfied by a perfectly fleshly human being, soon evaporates. An evanescence and indeterminacy of object usually seen as characterising the merely transitional phase of adolescence comes, in Flaubert, to imbue all human relations: this may be because so many of his characters suffer from what the psychologists used to call, in their grim phraseology, 'arrested development', or it may be because the object of love is by definition indeterminate: a repetition and / or an anticipation of loves past or yet to come.

If *November* shares these romantic themes with most of Flaubert's other juvenilia, it shows a new and much more mature approach to style. *November* moves from an 'I' narrative to a 'he' narrative, where an external narrator rounds off the Narrator's tale for him, putting his mal-du-siècle posing into place in no uncertain terms: Anthony Burgess compared the effect to a cold shower coming after the overheated erotic adolescent effusions that have preceded it, and other critics have suggested that Flaubert – soon to suffer the strange fit of illness, epileptic in character, that meant he could 'die' to the world, abandon his law studies and devote himself to writing – was killing off one aspect of himself, the solipsistic 'I', so as to rise anew as an objective, third-person artist. Be that as it may, *November* is much better written than *Memoirs of a Madman*, which in other ways prefigures it. 'Fragments in a Nondescript Style' reads the subtitle, with its fake modesty: the set-piece descriptions of climate and environment, and the almost hallucinatory exotic scenes dreamt up by the Narrator, already anticipate the mature novelist – though the Chateaubriand of the moody grandiloquence of *René* is also a strong influence. The young Flaubert seems at times to be practising his scales – a musical analogy which struck Sartre as particularly apt, given the euphoniousness of some of Flaubert's prose poetry. Sartre goes so far as to devote several detailed pages to the passage where the Narrator imagines his death while rounding the Cape, or succumbing to cholera in Calcutta: not only is the alliteration notably contrived, but the vowel sequence (in French: 'o-é-a-a-u-a') reminds Sartre of a symphony in A major. (The reader of an English translation should bear in mind that A major sounds quite different in French and in English.)

Sartre, indeed, is still the best analyst of the way Flaubert's whole career is implicit in his juvenilia. *November* is still an effusive text, all sunsets and vague immensities: but there are signs of the scrupulous attention to concrete reality (the details of the furnishings of Marie's room, for instance) that will mark the author of *Madame Bovary*. On the thematic level, Sartre brings out the ways in which Flaubert's bad faith, multiple evasions and passivity were the products of a social totality that Flaubert himself could not fully grasp: but he also, with something like amorous fascination, shows how Flaubert, by recording this constellation of failings so pitilessly, is one of the most lucid analysts of the syndrome that has come to be known as bovarysme. If Flaubert (like the Narrator of *November*) is indeed too passive, too much of a bystander to achieve Sartrean existential autonomy and commitment, he nonetheless chooses an activity – writing – which is, as it were, the engagement of the disengaged, the *vita activa* of the contemplative. And the politically engaged Sartre is also alert to the way the disengaged Flaubert, who to a large extent shared with the Narrator of *November* the temperament of a narcissistic dreamer, also went on to produce one of the most incisive political novels of the nineteenth (or indeed any other) century, *Sentimental Education*. Its protagonist Frédéric is, like the Narrator of *November*, another indecisive waverer, but he at least is forced to face a manifestation of political power at its most repressive as, in the 1851 *coup d'état*, the mounted dragoons of Louis Napoleon (soon to be enthroned as Emperor Napoleon III) come sweeping down the boulevards near the Paris Opéra while the crowd gazes on in mute terror. Frédéric does not understand this epiphany, perhaps, nor the magnificent (and / or stupid) sacrifice of his former friend the idealist Dussardier, who at least has found something to live and die for (he shouts '*Vive la République!*' and is cut down by Sénécal, another of Frédéric's old friends, now a lackey of the new regime). This seizure of power by Louis Napoleon took place on 2nd December. Given the

French predilection for labelling public upheavals by their months (the July Days of 1830, May '68…), we can say that Flaubert as an artist at least made the (in its way revolutionary) transition from *November* to December. The Frédéric of *Sentimental Education* is a character who does not just fade away, as the Narrator of *November* seems to, from *taedium vitae*, but has lived on – to encounter even graver challenges to male bourgeois solipsism and its romantic, world-weary posturing (or its suicidal depression). Which brings us back to *Manhattan*, for there is one item in Isaac's list of things that make life worth living which I deliberately left out – but it's there all the same, in between 'Swedish movies' and 'Marlon Brando', as Isaac acknowledges a text and an author who had already so accurately diagnosed his modern anhedonia, but also the world of history and change lying just beyond its comprehension: '*Sentimental Education*, by Flaubert'.

– *Andrew Brown, 2005*

Note on the Text:
I have used the text in Flaubert, *Oeuvres Complète*, vol. I, *Oeuvres de jeunesse*, ed. by Claudine Gothot-Mersch and Guy Sagnes (Paris: Gallimard, 'Pléiade', 2001).

November

'...*to indulge in foolery and fantastication.*'
Montaigne[1]

I love the autumn – that melancholy season that suits memories so well. When the trees have lost their leaves, when the sky at sunset still preserves the russet hue that fills with gold the withered grass, it is sweet to watch the final fading of the fires that until recently burnt within you.

I have just returned from my habitual walk across the empty meadows, along the cold ditches in whose waters the willows gaze on their reflections; the wind whistled through their bare branches, sometimes falling silent only to resume all of a sudden; then the little leaves still clinging to the bushes trembled anew, the grass shivered as its stalks bent down to the earth, and everything seemed to grow paler and icier; on the horizon the sun's disc melded into the overall whiteness of the sky, shedding around it a wan hint of fading vitality. I was cold and almost afraid.

I took shelter behind a grassy knoll; the wind had dropped. I don't know why, but as I sat on the ground, thinking of nothing and watching the smoke rise from the thatched roofs in the distance, my whole life rose up before me like a phantom, and the bitter fragrance of bygone days came back to me, with an odour of dried grass and dead trees; the years of my paltry life passed before me, as if swept along by winter's pitiful blast; some dread force drove them willy-nilly through my mind, with more fury than the gusts of wind chasing the leaves down the peaceful country paths; some strange irony brushed against them and turned them over for me to gaze at, and then they all flew off together and faded away into the overcast sky.

It's a gloomy season, this one – it is just as if life were about to depart with the sun. A shudder runs not just over your skin but through your heart, too; every sound fades away, the horizon grows faint and dim all around, and everything seems on the verge of sleep or death. Sometimes I would see the cows coming home, mooing at the setting sun; the lad driving them ahead of him with a bramble switch shivered in his coarse cotton clothes, and they slipped in the mud as they came down the hillside, trampling a few apples still left in the grass. The sun shed a final farewell from behind the hazy hills, the lights of the houses started to glimmer in the valley, and the moon, that luminary of dewdrops and tears, started to unveil herself from between the clouds, and to show forth her pallid face.

I savoured at length my wasted life; I told myself joyfully that my youth was over and done with – for it is a real joy to sense the chill creep into your heart, and to be able to say, prodding it like a still-smoking hearth, 'It's stopped burning'. I slowly went over everything in my life: ideas, passions, days of anger, days of grief, heartbeats of hope, heart-rending anguish. I saw it all again, like a man visiting the catacombs and gazing his fill at the lines of the dead laid out on either side of him, row upon row. And yet, if you merely count the years, I was born not all that long ago: but I have my own countless memories, and I am as weighed down by them as old men are weighed down by all the days that they have lived; it seems to me at times that I have been around for centuries and that my self contains the debris of a thousand former existences. Why should this be? Have I loved? Have I hated? Have I sought anything in particular? I am still full of doubt; I have lived far from all movement and all activity, and have never bestirred myself either for glory or for pleasure, for knowledge or for riches.

Nobody has known anything of what I am about to relate, not even those people who saw me every day. They were to me like the bed on which I sleep, and that knows nothing of my dreams. In any case, is a man's heart not a vast solitude where no one else ever ventures? The passions that penetrate it are like travellers in the Sahara Desert: they are stifled, and die, and their cries are not heard beyond its confines.

From my schooldays on, I was sad and bored, simmering with desires and filled with burning aspirations for a mindless and tumultuous existence; I dreamt up passions and longed to experience them all. Waiting for me, just beyond my twentieth year, lurked a whole world of bright lights and perfumes; life appeared to me, from afar, filled with radiance and a noise of triumph; as in a fairy tale I imagined great halls opening out one after another, with diamonds shimmering in the gleam of golden chandeliers; a name endowed with magical power is enough to make the enchanted gates swing open on their hinges, and as you step forward, your gaze is overwhelmed with magnificent vistas whose dazzle makes you smile and close your eyes.

Hazily, I yearned for something splendid that no words of mine could have expressed, nor any idea in my brain articulated, but for which I felt, nonetheless, a real and unremitting desire. I have always loved life's glitter. When I was a child, I would push my way through the crowd right up to the carriages of fairground hucksters to see the red braid of their servants and the ribbons on the bridles of their horses; I would linger for ages outside the tents of the jugglers, gazing at their baggy trousers and their embroidered ruffs. Ah, how I loved – more than anyone else – the girl on the tightrope, with her dangling ear-pendants swinging to and fro around her head, and her great necklace of precious stones jangling against her breast! How avidly I contemplated her, and how anxiously too, as she swung as high as the lamps that hung between the trees, and her dress, edged with golden spangles, flapped as she leapt, and billowed out in the air! Those were the first women I ever loved. My mind would whip itself into a frenzy thinking about those strange-shaped thighs, clad in pink tights, and those supple arms, swathed in rings that the dancers would clash together behind their backs when they bent over backwards so far that the plumes of their turbans touched the ground. I was already trying to imagine what woman was like (we think of women at every age: while still children, we fondle with a naive sensuality the breasts of those grown-up girls kissing us and cuddling us in their arms; at the age of ten, we dream of love; at fifteen, love comes along; at sixty, it is still with us, and if dead men in their tombs have any thought in their heads, it is how to make their way underground to the nearby grave, lift the shroud of the dear departed woman, and mingle with her in her sleep); thus, woman was an alluring mystery for me, one that troubled my poor childish head. From the feelings that arose in me when a woman happened to fix her gaze on me, I already sensed that there was something fateful in that arousing glance, something that causes men's willpower to melt – and it filled me simultaneously with fascination and fear.

What did I dream of during the long evenings of private study, when I would sit with my elbow propped on my desk, gazing at the wick of the oil lamp growing ever longer in the midst of the flame, and each drop of oil falling into the cup, while my schoolmates made their pens scrape across the paper, and every now and then came the sound of someone leafing through the pages of a book, or shutting it abruptly? I would make sure I finished my prep early, so I could indulge at leisure in these cherished musings. Indeed, I would hold the prospect before myself as a promise that contained all the allure of a real pleasure, and I would start by forcing myself to think of these visions like a poet intent on creating something and seeking to stimulate his inspiration; I would follow my thoughts as far as they would take me, I would examine them from every angle, I would plumb their depths, I would return to the surface, and then I would start all over again. Soon my unbridled imagination was hurtling forward, leaping with marvellous energy up and away from reality; I would devise adventures and spin out stories for myself, I would build my own palaces and take up residence in them like an emperor, I would dig out the diamonds from every mine and strew them in bucketfuls on the path along which I was to travel.

And when evening had fallen, and we are all lying in our white beds, with our white curtains around them, and there was only the duty master pacing up and down the dormitory, how much more deeply would I fold my thoughts within myself, joyfully hiding within my breast that bird whose wings were beating and whose warmth I could sense! I always took a long time getting to sleep, I would listen to the hours chiming – and the more hours that chimed, the happier I was; they seemed to be pushing me forth into the world as they sang out, and they greeted every moment of my life, telling me as they did so, 'Think of the others, the others, the others! Of what is to come! Farewell! Farewell!' And when the last vibration had died away, when my ear was no longer filled with its ringing, I would say to myself, 'Until tomorrow; the same hour will chime, but tomorrow it will be one day less, one day more towards that distant prospect, towards that gleaming goal, towards my future, towards that sun whose radiance is flooding through me, and that I will then be able to touch with my own hands,' and I told myself that it would be long in coming, and dozed off almost with tears in my eyes.

Certain words overwhelmed me, *woman* and *mistress* in particular; I would look for an explanation of the former in books, engravings, and paintings – whose draperies I longed to tear away so I could see whatever lay behind them. The day when I finally guessed at the full reality, I was at first beside myself with rapture, as if I had discovered some supreme harmony, but soon I calmed down and from then on I lived with greater joy, feeling an impulse of pride as I told myself that I was a man, a being formed for the purpose of one day having a woman of my own; the password to life was known to me, and this was almost as good as actually entering into life and tasting its delights; my desire went no further, and I was happy to remain satisfied with what I knew. As for a *mistress*, this for me was a satanic creature, and the magic of the mere name threw me into prolonged raptures: it was for their mistresses' sake that kings would ruin or conquer provinces, for them that Indian carpets were woven, gold was fashioned, marble chiselled, and the world set astir; a mistress has slaves, with plumed fans to drive away the flies, when she lies asleep on satin cushions; elephants laden with gifts wait for her to awaken, palanquins bear her softly to the fountain's edge, she is seated on a throne in a radiant and fragrant atmosphere, far from the crowd, which both execrates and idolises her.

This mystery of woman seen apart from marriage – and all the more feminine for that – nagged at me and tempted me with the twofold allure of love and riches. There was nothing I loved so much as the theatre, I even loved the buzz of conversation in the intervals, and the very corridors that I strode down, my heart beating with excitement, as I looked for my seat. When the performance had already started, I would run up the stairs; I could hear the sound of the instruments, voices and cries of 'bravo!', and when I entered,

when I sat down, all the air was imbued with the warm odour
of a well-dressed woman – a whiff of bouquets of violets, white
gloves, and embroidered handkerchiefs; the galleries,
thronged with people, resembled crowns of flowers and
diamonds that seemed to be hanging in suspense as they
listened to the singing; there was no one but the actress at the
foreground of the stage, and her breast, from whence emerged
a rapid cascade of notes, rose and fell with a quiver, as the
rhythm whipped her voice into a gallop and dragged it along
in a whirlwind of melody, while the roulades rippled through
her swelling throat, like a swan's, under a flurry of aerial kisses;
she would hold out her arms, cry aloud, weep, flicker and
flame, and summon the mysterious object of some inconceiv-
able love; and when she resumed the main theme, it was as if
she were tearing out my heart with the sound of her voice so as
to fuse it with her own being in a shudder of love.

The audience applauded her and threw her flowers, and,
in my transport, I savoured the crowd's adoration that rained
down on her, the love of all those men and the desire of each
and every one of them. She was the woman by whom I longed
to be loved, loved with an all-devouring and terrifying passion,
the love of a princess or an actress, the kind of love that makes
you swell with pride and immediately makes you the equal
of the rich and powerful! How beautiful she is, the woman
applauded and envied by all, the woman who allows the
crowd to indulge its dreams night after night, and fills it with
the fever of desire, the woman who appears only by the light of
the chandeliers, radiant and singing, and walking straight into
a poet's ideal vision as if it were a life made for her alone! For
the man who loves her she must invent another love, even
more splendid than the love she pours out in floods on all
those panting hearts that drink their fill from it! She must

have songs of even greater sweetness, and deeper notes, more passionate and tremulous! If only I could have drawn near those lips whence those melodies emerged so pure, and touch those gleaming locks of hair that shone under their pearls! But the footlights seemed to me a barrier between myself and the world of illusion; beyond it there lay the universe of love and poetry, where passions were more splendid and resonant, forests and palaces faded and vanished like smoke, sylphs descended from the heavens, and everything was alive with song and love.

This is what I dreamt of alone in the evenings, when the wind whistled down the corridors, or during the break, while the others were playing skittles or football, while I wandered along at the foot of the wall, crunching underfoot the leaves that had fallen from the lime trees so I could enjoy the sound of my feet scuffling and kicking through them.

Soon, the desire to love seized me. I yearned for love with a boundless longing, I dreamt of all its torments, I awaited at every instant some heart-rending passion that would fill me with overwhelming joy. Several times I thought I had found it; I would take into my arms the first attractive woman to come along, telling myself, 'She's the one I love!' But the memory of her that I wished to preserve grew pale and indistinct instead of growing stronger; in any case, I sensed that I was forcing myself to love, putting on an act, trying to deceive my own heart – in vain. As I came down to earth, I was overwhelmed by a prolonged sadness; I almost started to feel nostalgic for the loves I had not had, and then I dreamt up new ones in an attempt to fill the void in my soul.

It was the day after I had been to a ball or to the theatre, or on my return from a two- or three-day break, that I would dream up some passionate affair. I would picture the woman

I had chosen, exactly as I had seen her, in a white dress, swept along in a waltz on the arms of a dancing partner holding her in his arms and smiling at her, or else leaning on the velvet-topped ledge of a theatre box, serenely showing off her queenly profile. The din of the contredanses, and the dazzle and glitter of the lights, continued for a while to linger in my mind, then everything finally dissolved in the dull, aching monotony of a daydream. In this way I had a thousand little love affairs that lasted a week or a month, and that I would like to have prolonged for centuries; I do not know what bits and pieces I composed them from, nor what was the aim of all these vague desires; it was, I believe, the need for a new feeling, and an aspiration towards some lofty goal, whose summit always lay just out of sight.

The heart enters puberty before the body; I had a greater need to love than to enjoy the pleasures of the senses, and a greater longing for love than for physical satisfaction. These days, I cannot even remember the kind of love that I felt during my early adolescence, in which the senses play no part and which the infinite alone can satisfy; situated between childhood and youth, it is the transitional stage between them, and passes so quickly that it is soon forgotten.

I had read the word *love* so often in the works of the poets, and I said it over and over again to myself, and filled myself with the magic of its sweetness; as a result, at every star that twinkled in the blue sky of a warm night, at every gentle plash of the wave against the shore, at every sunbeam that glittered in the dewdrops I would tell myself, 'I'm in love! Ah, I'm in love!' – and this thought filled me happiness and pride. I was always on the verge of feeling the most tender devotion, especially when a woman brushed past me or looked me full in the face: then I yearned to love her a thousand times more, suffer even more intensely, so that the beating of my little heart might break my breast.

There is a certain age – you must remember it well, Reader – where you go around with a dreamy smile on your lips, as if the air were thronged with kisses; your heart swells in the fragrant breeze, and your blood pulses warm in your veins, fizzing through your body like sparkling wine in a crystal goblet. You awaken happier and richer than you were the night before, more aquiver with life and emotion; streams of honey flow round your body and fill you with an intoxicating warmth; trees bend and nod their heads sagely in the wind, the leaves rustle in serried throngs as if in avid conversation, the clouds glide along and, between them, the depths of the sky open up and reveal the smiling moon, gazing down on her reflection in the river. When you go for a walk in the evening, breathing in the odour of the mown hay, listening to the cuckoo calling in the woods, and watching the shooting stars, your heart is purer – as I'm sure you've felt – and even more suffused with air and light and sky-blue radiance than the serene horizon, where the earth gently and calmly kisses the heavens. Ah, the perfume that arises from women's hair! How soft is the skin of their hands, and how intense their gaze!

But I had already gone beyond those first dazzling impressions of childhood, those disquieting memories of former dreams. Now, I was entering into a *real* life in which I had my own place, a vast harmony in which my heart sang a hymn and thrilled in magnificent concord; I joyfully revelled in this blossoming delight, and my awakening senses intensified my pride. Like the first man ever to be created, I was finally stirring from a long slumber, and next to me I found a creature similar to me, but alluringly different enough to induce a dizzying force of attraction between us. Thereupon, I was filled with a new and glorious desire for this new shape, as the sun shone with even greater purity, the flowers wafted their fragrance more sweetly than ever, and the shade became even more intimate and inviting.

At the same time, I sensed that my intelligence was developing day by day, in harmony with my heart. I do not know whether my ideas were feelings, since they all had the same warmth as passions, and the inner delight I felt in the depths of my being overflowed out into the world and filled it with the sweet smell of my flooding happiness; I was about to experience the most intense of pleasures, and, like a man at his mistress' door, I took my time, deliberately forcing myself to wait, savouring my sure and certain expectation, and telling myself, 'Very soon I will be holding her in my arms, she will be mine, yes, mine – and not just in my dreams!'

What a strange paradox! I fled the society of women, and yet I took the greatest delight in their company; I claimed I did not love them in the least, while in fact I lived in all of them and longed to penetrate the essence of each of them, and melt into their beauty. Their lips, even now, were inviting me to kisses that were more than maternal; in my thoughts I would enfold myself in their hair and lie between their breasts, crushed in a divine and smothering embrace; I longed to be the necklace that caressed their necks, the bodice hook that bit into their shoulders, the garments that covered the rest of their bodies. Beyond their clothes I could see no further; hidden beneath was an infinitude of love, and I lost myself in contemplation of it.

Those passions that I yearned to experience were things I could study in books. As far as I was concerned, human life circled round two or three ideas, two or three words, and everything else rotated around these like a satellite around its star. In this way, I had peopled my infinite with countless golden suns; love stories lodged in my mind next to great revolutions, and splendid passions rubbed shoulders with great crimes. I would dream simultaneously of the star-filled nights of tropical countries and of sacked cities going up in flames, of the creepers of virgin forests and the pomp of long-dead monarchies, of cradles and of graves; waves murmuring in the rushes, turtle doves cooing in the dovecotes, myrtle woods and the scent of aloes, swords clashing on armour, horses champing at the bit, the gleam of gold, all of life's glitter, the agony of the dying – I would contemplate it all with the same open-mouthed gaze, as if it had been an anthill seething at my feet. But from this life, so restless on the surface, and echoing with such a hubbub of discordant cries, there arose an immense bitterness that fused all these things ironically together.

On winter evenings, I would pause before the lit windows of houses where a dance was being held, and I would watch the shadows moving behind the red curtains; I could hear noises richly indicative of luxury – the clink of glasses on trays, the clatter of silverware in dishes; and I told myself that it was perfectly possible for me to join in these thronged festivities, this banquet where everyone was eating his fill; a wild pride stopped me from doing so, since I found that my aloofness made me look attractive, and that my heart was so much nobler for shunning all men's joys. So I would continue walking through the deserted streets, where the street lamps swung on their chains with a melancholy creak.

I dreamt of the pain suffered by the poets, I felt their sorrows as they shed glittering tears, and shared them in the depths of my heart – I was overwhelmed by them, distraught; sometimes, the empathy they inspired in me seemed to make me their equal, and raised me to their level; pages they had written that left other readers cold would send me into raptures, and give me the prophetic fury of the Pythian goddess. I would inflict these pages on my mind as and when I wanted; I would recite them by the seashore, or walk through the grass, my head bowed, repeating them to myself in the most tender and amorous tone of voice.

Woe betide him who has never longed to break out in tragic wrath, and does not know by heart lines of love poetry that he can recite to himself in the moonlight! It is wonderful to live in eternal beauty like this, to drape oneself in the mantle of kings, to have at one's beck and call passions at the highest pitch of their expression, and to love loves that genius has rendered immortal.

From that time forth, my life was a great and boundless ideal; hovering in free and easy tranquillity, I would fly like a bee gathering my nourishment and sustenance from everything I encountered. I tried to discover, in the rumour of forests and waves, words that other men could not hear, and I pricked up my ears to listen to the revelation of their harmony; from the clouds and the sun I would compose huge paintings, which no language could ever translate; and in human activities too, I would suddenly perceive similarities and contrasts whose luminous precision dazzled even myself. Sometimes art and poetry seemed to open up their endless horizons to me, illuminating each other with their own radiance; I would build palaces of warm glowing copper, and mount ever upwards into a radiant sky, on a staircase of clouds softer than eiderdown.

The eagle is a proud bird, which perches on lofty peaks; beneath him he sees the clouds rolling through the valleys, drawing the swallows in their train; he sees the rain falling on the fir trees, great blocks of marble crashing down into the mountain streams, the shepherd whistling his goats along, and the chamois leaping from crag to crag. The rain comes pelting down, the storm blasts the trees, the torrents cascade with a noise like a sob, the waterfall smokes and rebounds, the thunder roars and crashes into the mountain peak, but all in vain; he serenely soars above the scene, beating his wings; the hullabaloo on the mountain merely entertains him; he utters cries of joy, does battle with the scudding clouds, and mounts ever higher into his immense sky.

I too derived entertainment from the noise of tempests and the vague hubbub of men rising up to me; I lived in a lofty eyrie, where my heart swelled with pure air, and I uttered shrieks of triumph so as to stave off the boredom of my solitude.

I was very quickly overcome by an entrenched disgust for the things of this life. One morning, I felt as if I were old, and sated with the experience of a thousand things I had never lived through; I was indifferent towards even the most alluring of them, and felt disdain for the most splendid; everything that other men longed for seemed to me to be pitiable, I could not see a single thing worthy of a moment's desire – perhaps it was my very vanity that made me feel above ordinary vanity, and perhaps my detachment was merely the excess of a boundless greed. I was like those new buildings on which moss already starts to grow before they are finished; the boisterous joys of my schoolmates bored me, and I would shrug at their sentimental twaddle: some of them would hold on for a whole year to an old white glove or a withered camellia, lavishing kisses and sighs on it; others would write to milliners, or arrange trysts with kitchen maids; the former struck me as idiotic, the latter as grotesque. And then, I was equally bored by both good and bad society; I was cynical with the devout and mystical with libertines. As a result, nobody liked me very much at all.

At that period, when I was still a virgin, I enjoyed staring at prostitutes. I would pass through the streets they lived on, and hang around wherever they plied their trade; sometimes I would speak to them, exposing myself to temptation; I followed them around, touched them, and entered the atmosphere they weave around themselves; and, impudent young fellow that I was, I believed I was keeping a cool head – I felt that my heart was empty, but it was the emptiness of the abyss.

I loved to lose myself in the swirling eddy of the streets. Sometimes I would indulge in some stupid pastime, such as staring fixedly at every passer-by to discover on his face some vice or dominant passion. All those faces swept by me: some were smiling, and whistled as they headed away, their hair fluttering in the wind; others were pale, others red, yet others livid; they swiftly disappeared past me, slipping away one after the other like shop and tavern signs you see when riding along in a cab. Or else I merely watched the feet hurrying along in every direction, and tried to link each foot to a body, each body to an idea, and all these movements to their different goals; I wondered where all these steps were heading, and why all these people were hurrying by. I watched carriages rumbling into gates, as the columned porticoes echoed, and I heard the clatter of the heavy carriage-step being let down. Crowds thronged the theatre entrances; I watched the lights glimmering through the fog, and, high above, the black and starless sky; at one street corner, there was an organ-grinder playing, while children in rags sang, and a fruit seller trundled his cart along, lit up with a red lantern; the cafés were filled with uproar, the ices glistened in the light of the gas lamps, and the knives glittered on the marble-topped tables; the poor gathered at the door, shivering and standing on tiptoes to watch the rich eat; I would mingle with them, and join them as they gazed at those whom life has blessed; I envied them their vulgar joy, since there are days when you are so sad that you long to make yourself even sadder, and you willingly plunge ever deeper into a facile despair, your heart swollen with tears as you force yourself into a fit of weeping. I've often wanted to be a wretched, ragged pauper, to be tormented by hunger pangs, to feel the blood pouring from a wound, and to have some cause of hatred so I can wreak my revenge.

What, then, is this nagging disquiet? We are as proud of it as we are proud of our genius, and we conceal it like some secret love. We tell it to nobody, we keep it for ourselves alone, we hug it to our chests with tearful kisses. And yet, what is there to complain of? And what makes us so gloomy at an age when everything smiles on us? Don't we have devoted friends? A family of which we are the pride and joy, patent-leather boots, a nice padded jacket? All these great nameless sorrows are poetic rhapsodies, memories from our unedifying readings, figures of rhetorical hyperbole – but then, maybe happiness too is a metaphor invented on a day of boredom? I have often doubted this, but nowadays I have no doubt at all.

I have never loved anything, and yet I so longed to love! I will have to die without ever enjoying anything really nice. And now, human life itself still holds out countless facets that I have barely glimpsed: to take just one example, never have I sat on a panting horse by the side of a spring and heard the sound of the horn in the depths of the woods; never, on a warm night filled with the odour of roses, have I felt a friendly hand grasp mine in tremulous silence. Ah, I am emptier, sadder and more vacant than a staved-in barrel whose contents have all been drunk, and on which the spiders weave their webs in the darkness.

Mine was neither the sorrow of René nor the vast heavenly expanse of his troubles, more splendid and silvery than the moon's rays; I was neither chaste like Werther nor debauched like Don Juan; I was neither pure enough nor strong enough for anything.[2]

Thus I was exactly what all of you are – a certain man, living, sleeping, eating, drinking, laughing, wrapped up in himself and finding within himself, wherever he goes, the same ruined hopes, dashed the moment they are born, the same dust from things crushed to smithereens, the same paths trodden countless times, the same unexplored, terrible and dreary depths. Are you not tired as I am of waking up every morning and seeing the sun all over again? Tired of living the same life, suffering the same sorrow? Tired of desiring, and tired of being sated? Tired of waiting, and tired of possessing?

What's the point of writing this? Why should I continue, in the same doleful voice, to relate the same dismal tale? When I began it, I knew that it was a fine story, but as I proceed with it, my tears fall onto my heart and drown my voice.

Oh, the pale winter sun! It's as sad as a memory of happiness. The shadows are all around us; let us gaze into the fire in our hearth; a great tangled web of flames seems to glow between the rows of coals, and to beat like veins pulsating with another life; let us wait for night to fall.

Let us remember our good days, high-spirited and com-panionable days when the sun shone, and hidden birds sang once the rain had stopped; days when we went out for a stroll round the garden; the sand on the paths was damp, the corollas of the roses had fallen into the flower-beds, and the air was filled with fragrance. Why didn't we make the most of our happiness while we still held it in our hands? On such days we really should have made an effort to enjoy life and savour each minute at length, so that it would last longer; and there were indeed days that passed by like others, and which I can still remember with delight. Once, for instance, one cold winter's day, we had come back from a walk and, as there weren't very many of us, we were allowed to sit down round the stove; we stretched out and warmed ourselves, toasting our hunks of bread on our rulers, as the stovepipe hummed and buzzed; swe talked about countless things: the plays we had seen, the women we loved, the time when we would leave school, what we'd do when we grew up, etc. On another occasion, I spent the whole afternoon lying on my back, in a field where there were some little daisies just poking out of the grass; they were yellow and white, and melded into the green of the meadow, making a carpet of infinitely subtle hues; the pure sky was covered with little white clouds rippling like rounded waves; I covered my face with my hands and gazed through them at the sun, which made the edges of my fingers glow golden and turned my flesh pink; I deliberately shut my eyes tight and saw, behind my eyelids, great green blotches fringed with gold. And, one evening, I don't remember when, I had drowsed off to sleep at the foot of a haystack; when I awoke, night had fallen, the stars were twinkling, the haystacks cast lengthy shadows, and the moon had a lovely silvery face.

How long ago it all was! Was *I* living at that time? Was it really me? It is me now? Each minute of my life finds itself suddenly separated from the preceding one by an abyss; between yesterday and today there is an eternity that fills me with terror; every day it seems to me that I was less wretched the day before and, without being able to say what else I then possessed, I am sure that I am growing ever poorer, and that each hour as it comes takes something from me. I am just amazed that there is still room in my heart for suffering; but man's heart is an inexhaustible reservoir of melancholy: one or two moments of happiness fill it to the brim, but all the many miseries of humanity can easily congregate and find lodgings in it together.

If you had asked me what it was I needed, I wouldn't have been able to tell you; my desires had no specific object, and my sadness had no immediate cause; or rather, there were so many objects and so many causes that I wouldn't have been able to isolate a single one of them. All the passions crammed into my heart and became entrapped there; they set each other aflame, as if in concentric mirrors. I was a modest person, yet full of pride; a solitary, who dreamt of glory. Shunning society, I yet had a burning ambition to appear on its stage and cut a dash; though chaste, day and night I would abandon myself in my dreams to the most unbridled lusts, the fiercest pleasures. The life that I held pent up inside me congealed within my heart, and choked it.

Sometimes, at the end of my tether, devoured by boundless passions, filled with the burning lava that flowed from my soul, filled with a furious love for nameless things, overcome by nostalgic longing for magnificent dreams, tempted by all the intense pleasures of thought, embracing all poetry and all harmony, and crushed beneath the weight of my heart and my pride, I would fall, shattered, into an abyss of pain; the blood rushed to my face, my arteries pounded deafeningly, my breast seemed about to break, I could no longer see, I could no longer feel, I was drunk, I was mad, I imagined that I was a great man, I imagined that I harboured some supreme incarnation, the revelation of which would fill the world with amazement – and when this incarnation felt itself being torn apart, this was the very life of the god I bore within my entrails. To that magnificent god I sacrificed every hour of my youth; I had made of myself a temple to contain something divine, but the temple remained empty, nettles have grown between the stones, the pillars are crumbling, and now the owls are making their nests within it. I did not take advantage of my existence, and so my existence took advantage of me, and wore me down; my dreams drained my energies more than any great labour; an entire creation, motionless, unaware of itself, led a secret and subdued life under the surface of my own; I was a sleeping chaos of countless fecund principles that did not know how to manifest themselves, or what to do with themselves; they were seeking their proper shape and awaiting the mould in which they could be cast.

I was, in the variety of my being, like an immense jungle in India, where life throbs in every atom and appears, monstrous or adorable, in every ray of sunlight; the azure sky is filled with perfumes and poisons; tigers leap, elephants tread proudly like living pagodas, gods, mysterious and deformed, lurk in the depths of caves among great heaps of gold; and, through the middle of it all flows the broad river, with open-jawed crocodiles slapping their scales against the lotus on the river-bank, and its islands of flowers that the current sweeps away together with tree trunks and corpses turned rotten and green by the plague. And yet I loved life, but only when it was expansive, radiant, gleaming; I loved it in the furious gallop of warhorses, in the glitter of the stars, in the movement of the waves as they hasten to the shore; I loved it in the quiver of sweet bare breasts, in the tremulousness of loving glances, in the vibration of violin strings, in the shimmering of oak trees, in the setting sun which fills the windows with its gold and makes you think of the balconies of Babylon on which queens used to lean as they gazed across Asia.

And amidst all this I remained immobile; between all those activities unfolding before my eyes – activities that I deliberately provoked – I remained inactive, as inert as a statue surrounded by a swarm of flies buzzing round its ears and scampering across its marble surface.

Oh, how intensely I would have loved, if I *had* loved – if I had been able to concentrate on one single point all those divergent forces that assembled within me! Sometimes, I would have given anything to find a woman; I longed to love her, she meant the world to me, I expected everything from her, she was my sun of poetry who would make every flower blossom and every beauty gleam resplendent; I promised myself a divine love, and endowed her in advance with a halo so bright it dazzled me; and the first woman who came towards me, by chance, through the crowd, was the woman to whom I vowed my soul, and I shot her a significant glance so that she would easily understand me, would read my entire being from this single glance, and love me. I placed my destiny in the hands of this chance encounter, but she passed by like all the others, like the last ones and the next ones, and then I would come down to earth, in a sorrier state than a torn sail drenched by the storm.

After such moments of delirium, life resumed, opening out onto the eternal monotony of its passing hours and its repetitive days; I would await the evening impatiently, counting how many evenings there still remained before the end of the month; I wished it was already the next season, which I could see smiling with the promise of a better life. Sometimes, to shake off this leaden mantle that weighed down on my shoulders, and keep my head busy with science and ideas, I tried to work, to read; I would open a book, and then two books, and then ten, and without having read two lines of a single one of them, I would throw them down in disgust and fall back into my somnolent boredom.

What are we supposed to do here on earth? What should we dream of? What should we build? Tell me, then, you who find life entertaining, you who march towards a goal and torment yourself to achieve some particular aim!

I thought nothing good enough for me, and, in the same way, I thought myself good for nothing. To work, to sacrifice everything for an idea, for an ambition, a wretched and trivial ambition, to have a position, a name?... And then? What's the use! Anyway, I didn't like fame, and the most resounding acclaim would never have satisfied me since it would never have harmonised perfectly with my heart's longings.

I was born longing to die. Nothing seemed to me more utterly foolish than life, or more shameful than to care two pins for it. Brought up without a religion, like all the men of my age, I had neither the cut and dried happiness of the atheists, nor the ironical insouciance of the sceptics. If I did, doubtless on a mere whim, sometimes go into a church, it was to listen to the organ, to admire the stone statuettes in their niches; but as for dogma, I didn't take a single step towards accepting it; I felt myself to be a true son of Voltaire.

I could see other people living, but with a life different from mine: some believed, others denied, others doubted, yet others didn't bother their heads with any of all this and just attended to their business, in other words sold their wares in their shops, wrote their books, or expostulated from their pulpits; this was 'mankind', as they call it, a restless surge of wicked, cowardly, idiotic and ugly men. And I was part of the crowd, like a piece of seaweed swept along by the ocean, lost in the midst of the numberless waves that rolled and roared on every side around me.

I would like to have been an emperor, for the sake of his absolute power, his many slaves, and his armies, all filled with delirious dedication to him; I would like to have been a woman for the sake of her beauty, to be able to admire myself, strip myself naked, let my hair fall down to my heels and gaze on my reflection in the streams. I would lose myself whenever I wanted in boundless daydreams; I imagined I was participating in splendid ancient festivities, a king of the Indies out hunting on a white elephant, watching Ionian dances, listening to the Greek waves plashing on the steps of a temple, listening to the night breezes in the oleanders of my gardens, and taking flight with Cleopatra on my ancient galley. Ah! What madness! Woe betide the gleaner as she abandons her task and raises her head to see the berlin carriages rumbling down the highway! When she settles back to work, she will dream of cashmere and the love of princes, she won't be able to find a single ear of corn, and will return home without having gathered her sheaf.

It would have been better to do what everyone else does, neither taking life too seriously nor seeing it as merely grotesque, choosing a profession and practising it, grabbing one's share of the common cake, eating it and saying, 'It's delicious!' rather than following the gloomy path that I have trodden all alone; then I wouldn't be here writing this, or at least it would have been a different story. The further I proceed with it, the more confused it seems even to me, like hazy prospects seen from too far away, since everything passes, even the memory of our most scalding tears and our heartiest laughter; our eyes soon dry, our mouths resume their habitual shape; the only memory that remains to me is that of a long tedious time that lasted for several winters, spent in yawning and wishing I were dead.

Perhaps that's the reason why I thought I was a poet; none of the requisite miseries was lacking, as – alas! – you can see. Yes, once upon a time I thought I had genius, I strode along with my head crammed with magnificent thoughts, style flowed from my pen as easily as the blood flowed through my veins; at the least brush with beauty, a pure melody would rise within me, like those aerial voices, those sounds formed by the wind, that waft from the mountains; human passions would have vibrated in marvellous sympathy if I had only touched them, my head was full of dramas all ready and waiting, with many scenes of furious passion and repressed anguish; from the child in its cradle to the dead man in his coffin, humanity echoed within me; sometimes, gigantic ideas would dart across my mind like those great mute flashes of summer lightning that illuminate a whole city, with all the details of its buildings and all its street corners and crossroads. I was shaken and dazzled; but when I discovered that other people had already had the same thoughts, and expressed them in the very same way that I had conceived for them, I promptly fell into a bottomless slough of discouragement; I had imagined myself to be their equal, and I was merely their copyist! Thereupon I would pass from the intoxication of genius to the desolate sense of mediocrity, with all the rage of dethroned kings and all the torments of shame. There were days on which I would have sworn I was born for the Muse, while at other times I felt I was practically an idiot; and constantly passing in this way from such heights to such depths, I ended up, like everyone who has been both rich and poor many times in his life, being and remaining thoroughly wretched.

Throughout that time, each morning as I awoke it seemed to me that some great event was about to occur that very day;

my heart was big with hope, as if I had been expecting a cargo of happiness to come in from some distant land; but as the day went by, my morale would sink; at dusk, in particular, I clearly saw that nothing would ever come. Finally, night fell and I went to bed.

Plaintive harmonies arose between physical nature and myself. How my heart would contract when the wind whistled through the keyholes, when the street lamps shed their light on the snow, when I heard the dogs howling at the moon!

I could see nothing to which I could cling, either society or solitude, poetry, knowledge, impiety or religion; I wandered round amidst them all, like the souls which hell has rejected and which paradise disdains. Then I would fold my arms, regarding myself as a dead man; I was now nothing but a mummy embalmed in my sorrow; fate, which had weighed down on me since my youth, now extended to the entire world, I could see it active and manifest in all human actions, just as universally as the sun shining over the earth's surface; fate became a dreadful deity, which I adored as the Indians adore the mobile colossus that rolls over their bellies.[3] I wallowed in my gloom, which I now did not even try to evade; indeed, I savoured it, with the despairing joy of the patient scratching his wound and laughing when he sees the blood on his fingernails.

I was seized by a nameless rage against life, against men, against everything. My heart was a treasure-house of tenderness, and yet I became fiercer than tigers; I longed to annihilate creation and join it in an endless slumber of nothingness – if only I could have awoken to see the flames of sacked cities! I yearned to hear the cracking of bones in the crackling fire, to cross rivers clogged with corpses, to gallop over entire subjugated peoples and crush them beneath my horse's hooves – to be Genghis Khan, Tamerlane, Nero, able to shed terror across the world with a mere frown.

The more exultant and visionary I became, the more I shut myself away and turned inward. My heart dried up long ago, nothing new ever enters it now, it's as empty as the tombs in which the dead have rotted away. I had grown to hate the sun, I was exasperated by the sound of rivers and the sight of woods, nothing seemed to me more utterly inane than the countryside; everything became melancholy and insignificant, I lived in a perpetual twilight.

Sometimes I would ask myself if I wasn't mistaken; I would consider my youth and my future, but what a pitiful youth, and what an empty future!

When I wanted to stop brooding over the spectacle of my own misery and turn my gaze out to the world, what I could see of it was howls, cries, tears, convulsions, the same old play being put on again and again by the same old actors. 'To think that there are people who study it all,' I said to myself, 'and who settle back down to work every morning!' Only some great love might have rescued me from my plight, but I regarded that as a thing not of this world, and I bitterly regretted the loss of all the happiness I had dreamt of.

Then death appeared to me in all its allure. I have always loved death; as a child, I longed for it simply so as to know it, to find out what lies within the grave, and in that sleep what dreams may come; I remember how I would often scrape the verdigris off old coins to poison myself, or try to swallow pins, or go to an attic window to hurl myself down into the street... When I reflect that almost all children do likewise, and play at suicide, I can't help but think that man, whatever he may say, has a raging love for death. He gives to death all that he creates, he emerges from it and returns to it, he does nothing but dream of it all his life long, he contains its seeds within his body, and he harbours a yearning for it within his heart.

It is so pleasant to imagine that you no longer exist! It is so peaceful in cemeteries! There, as you lie full length, wrapped in your shroud, your arms crossed on your breast, the centuries pass by and no more awaken you than does the wind as it passes over the grass. How often have I stood in cathedral chapels gazing at those long stone statues lying on their tombs! Their calm is so profound that life here below has nothing like it to offer; on their cold lips there seems to hover a smile that has risen from the depths of the grave; they look as if they were asleep, and savouring death. To have no more cause for tears, to have experienced the last of those breakdowns when it seems that everything is cracking up like worm-eaten scaffolding – that is the happiness above all other happiness, the joy that needs no tomorrow, the dream that has no awakening. And then, perhaps, we go into a better world, beyond the stars, where we live on the life of light and fragrance; perhaps we are a part of the odour of roses and the freshness of meadows! Ah, no, no! I prefer to think that we are quite dead, that nothing emerges from the coffin; and if we must still experience anything, let it be our own nothingness, let death feed on itself and admire itself; just enough life to sense that we have ceased to be.

And I would climb to the tops of towers, I would lean over the abyss, I would wait as the vertigo mounted; I had an indescribable longing to fling myself off, to fly through the air, to evaporate into the winds; I would gaze at the points of daggers and the muzzles of pistols, I would put them to my forehead, and grow accustomed to the contact of their cold sharp edge; on other occasions, I would watch as wagoners turned round street corners and the huge wide wheels crushed the dust on the paving, reflecting that my head would be well and truly crushed underneath them as the horses trotted along. But I didn't want to be buried – the coffin terrifies me; I'd rather be laid on a bed of dried leaves, in the depths of the woods, so that my body could be gradually dispersed by the beaks of birds and the heavy showers of rain.

One day, in Paris, I was hanging around on the Pont-Neuf; it was winter, the Seine was full of drift ice, great round blocks of ice slowly floated along with the current and crashed together under the arches; the river water was greenish-hued, and I thought of all those who had come here to end it all. How many people had passed by the place where I now was, rushing along head first towards love or business affairs, only to return, one day, walking slowly and shakily, trembling at the approach of death! They went over to the parapet, they climbed up, and jumped. Oh, how much misery has ended here, and how much happiness begun! What a cold, damp grave! How it opens wide to receive all comers! How many there are in it! There they all are, in the depths, rolling slowly along with their contorted faces and their limbs blue with cold; each of these glacial waves bears them away as they slumber, and carries them gently down to sea.

Sometimes old men would cast envious glances at me, telling me I was lucky to be young, that this was the best age to be; their hollow eyes admired my white brow, they remembered their love affairs and told me all about them; but I often asked myself whether, in their day, life hadn't been more splendid, and since I couldn't see anything to envy in myself, I felt jealous at their nostalgia, since it concealed a happiness I had never known. And then I had all the pitiable quirks of a man in second childhood! I would laugh softly to myself, for hardly any reason at all, like people convalescing. Sometimes I would be overwhelmed by tenderness for my dog, and I would give him a big hug; or I'd go and look at some old school clothes in a cupboard, and think of the day I'd first worn them, the places they had been with me, and I would lose myself in memories of all my bygone days. For memories can be sweet, sad or cheerful – what difference does it make! Indeed, the most melancholy ones are the most delectable – do they not contain the infinite? We can sometimes spend centuries in exhaustive recollection of a certain hour that will never return, that has passed, that has forever ceased to exist, and that we would gladly give our whole future to get back.

But those memories are flaming torches arranged here and there in some great dim hall, gleaming in the murk; only by their glimmer can you see anything at all; what is near them is brightly lit, while everything else is darker, covered over with shadows and gloom.

Before going any further, I need to tell you the following story.

I don't remember exactly what year it was, but during one vacation I woke up in a good mood and looked out of the window. Day was dawning, the great white moon was rising up into the sky; between the steep-rounded hills, grey and pink wisps of vapour rose in a gentle haze and melded into the air; the hens in the yard were clucking. Behind the house, along the path that leads out to the fields, I heard a wagon pass by, its wheels rumbling and scraping through the ruts; it was the gleaners setting off to work. There was dew on the hedgerows, the sun was shining down from the sky, you could smell the water and the grass.

I left the house and headed for X***; I had three leagues to cover, and set off alone, without a stick, without a dog. First I walked along the paths that wind between the fields of wheat, and under the apple trees, along the hedgerows; I didn't have a thought in my head, I just listened to the sound of my own footsteps, and the rhythm of my movements rocked my musings. I was free, silent and calm, the weather was warm; from time to time I would stop; the pulse was beating in my temples, the crickets were chirping in the stubble; then I set off again. I came to a hamlet where there was nobody around, the yards were silent, it was a Sunday, I believe; the cows, sitting in the grass, in the shadow of the trees, were ruminating tranquilly, flicking their ears to chase away the midges. I remember walking along a path where a stream was flowing over pebbles, and green lizards and insects with golden wings slowly came up along the edges of the sunken road that was overgrown with foliage.

Then I found myself on a plateau, in a mown field; I had the sea ahead of me, it was bright blue, the sun shed over it a profusion of gleaming pearls, and furrows of fire ran through the waves; between the azure sky and the darker blue of the sea the horizon shone in flaming splendour; the vault of the heavens rose over my head and then sank behind the waves that rose up to meet it as if to close the circle of an invisible infinitude. I lay down in a furrow and gazed at the sky, lost in the contemplation of its beauty.

The field I found myself in was a wheat field; I could hear quails winging round me and darting down onto clods of earth; the sea was calm, and murmured more like a sigh than a voice; the sun itself seemed to be making its own sound, it flooded everything, its rays burnt my limbs, the earth mirrored its heat back to me, I was drenched in its light, I shut my eyes and could still see it. The smell of the waves rose all the way up to me, with the odour of kelp and marine plants; sometimes the waves seemed to stand still, or else they came to expire soundlessly on the foam-festooned shore, like lips giving a mute kiss. Then, in the silence between two waves, while the swelling ocean was quiet, I listened for a moment to the song of the quails, then the noise of the waves began again, and after that the noise of the birds.

I ran down to the seashore, across the mass of fallen rocks over which I leapt sure-footedly; I raised my head in pride, and boldly breathed in the fresh breeze that was drying my sweat-drenched hair; the spirit of God filled me, I felt my heart swell, and some strange impulse of adoration seized me; I longed to be absorbed in the sunlight and lose myself in that azure immensity, with the odour that arose from the surface of the waves; and then I was overwhelmed by a delirious joy, and I started to walk as if all the bliss of heaven had entered into my soul. As the cliff formed a promontory just here, the whole coast disappeared and I could see nothing but the sea: its breakers swept up over the pebbles to my feet, and foamed on the rocks that just broke the surface, beating rhythmically against them, enfolding them as if with liquid arms or a transparent film, then falling back again, lit up by a blue sheen; the wind blew up flecks of foam around me and stirred the surface of the rock pools that had formed in the hollows of the stones, the kelp wept and rocked up and down, still driven along by the momentum of the wave that had deposited it there; from time to time, a seagull would pass over with a vigorous beat of its wings, and soar up to the cliff top. As the sea withdrew, and its roar also diminished like a refrain fading away, the shore came closer, leaving open to view on the sand the furrows that the wave had traced. And then I understood all the happiness of creation and all the joy that God has prepared in it for mankind; nature seemed to me as beautiful as a complete harmony audible only to an ecstatic ear; I sensed something as tender as love and as pure as prayer rising from the depths of the horizon, and sweeping down from the heights of heaven to the tops of the ragged rocks; from the roar of the ocean and the light of day, something exquisite took shape, which I made my own as if it were a celestial domain; I felt myself to be really alive, happy and great, like the eagle who can stare at the sun and soar up into its beams.

Then everything seemed to me beautiful on earth, where I could see nothing disparate or bad; I loved everything, even the stones that jagged against my feet, even the sharp rocks on which I leant my hands, even that insensible nature that I imagined as hearing and loving me. And then I reflected how lovely it was, in the evening, to fall to one's knees and sing canticles at the foot of a Madonna shining in the candlelight, and to love the Virgin Mary, who appears to sailors, in a corner of the sky, holding the sweet child Jesus in her arms.

Then it was all over. All too soon I remembered that I was alive; I came back to my senses and started to walk away, sensing that I was again falling prey to the curse, returning to the human state; life had come back to me, as if to numbed and frozen limbs, as a sensation of suffering; and just as I had been filled with an unutterable happiness, I now fell into an indescribable depression, and I went to X***.

I came back home that evening, passing through the same paths; I spotted the tracks I had left on the sand and the place where I had lain down in the grass; it was as if I had dreamt it all. There are days on which you live twice over, the second existence being nothing but the memory of the first, and I kept coming to a halt in my path, facing a bush, a tree, a corner of the road, as if at that spot, that very morning, some great event in my life had taken place.

When I reached home, it was almost night, they'd shut the doors, and the dogs all started to bark.

The ideas of pleasure and love that had assailed me at the age of fifteen came back again at eighteen. If you have understood anything at all of what you have just read, you will remember that at that age I was still a virgin and had never been in love: as far as the beauty of the passions and their sonorous commotion were concerned, the poets provided me with themes for my reverie; as for the pleasures of the senses, those joys of the body so lusted after by adolescents, I stirred up an incessant desire for them in my heart by every kind of deliberate mental stimulation; just as those who are in love long to be able to put their love behind them by yielding ceaselessly to its charm, and to get rid of it by thinking about it constantly, it seemed to me that my thought alone would manage to drain that subject dry, quite unaided, emptying the cup of temptation by drinking from it. But, forever coming back to the same place I had started, I was trapped within a magic circle, and constantly bumping my head against it, longing for more room and freedom; at night, no doubt, I would dream of the most beautiful things of which one can dream, since in the morning my heart was filled with smiles and delightful presentiments; I was sorry to awaken, and I awaited impatiently for sleep to return, so that it could again give me those tremulous joys which filled my thoughts all day long, which I could have obtained that very moment had I so wished, and for which I felt a kind of religious awe.

It was then that I clearly sensed the demon of the flesh living in every muscle of my body, and coursing through my every vein; I pitied the innocent period when I had trembled under the gaze of women, when I would swoon over paintings or statues; I wanted to live, to enjoy, to love, I hazily realised that my hot season was arriving, just as in the first days of sunshine the ardour of summer is conveyed to you on the warm winds, although there is still no grass, nor leaves or roses. What should you do? Whom should you love? Who will love you? Who will be the great lady who will accept you? Which superhuman beauty will hold out her arms to you? Who can relate all the melancholy walks you take alone by the streams, all the sighs from swelling hearts that have risen up towards the stars on those stifling nights when you can barely breathe for the heat!

To dream of love is to dream of everything; it is the infinitude of happiness, the mystery within joy. With what ardour, oh you lovely, triumphant women, does our gaze devour you, and with what intensity do our eyes fasten on your faces! Grace and corruption emanate from each of your movements, the folds of your dresses rustle and stir us to the depths of our being, and from the surface of your bodies there wafts a certain something that kills us and enraptures us.

Henceforth, there was one word that seemed to me the most beautiful of all human words: the word *adultery*. An exquisite enchantment hovers hazily over it, and a singular magic fills it with fragrance; all the stories we tell, all the books we read, every move we make, all describe it and endlessly gloss it to the young man's heart; he drinks it in at will, finding in it the highest poetry – a mixture of malediction and pleasure.

It was in particular as spring approached, when the lilacs begin to bloom and the birds to sing amid the first leaves, that I felt my heart overwhelmed with a need to love, to melt completely away into love, to be absorbed in some great sweet emotion, and even to remake itself, so to speak, in light and fragrance. Even now, every year, for a few hours, I again experience this virginal feeling as it blossoms like a new bud; but joys do not flower again as do roses, and there is no more greenery left in my heart than there is on the highway, where the hot, dry wind tires your eyes and the dust swirls in rising spirals.

However, now that I am about to tell you the following tale, on the verge of digging down into this memory, I tremble and draw back; it's just as if I were about to visit some former mistress. Your heart is oppressed, and you halt on every step of the staircase, frightened at the idea of meeting her again, and yet afraid she might not be there. The same goes for certain ideas with which you have lived for too long; you'd like to get rid of them once and for all, and yet they flow through you like life itself, and your heart breathes them in as if they were its natural atmosphere.

I've told you I loved the sun; on the days when it shone, my soul would enjoy something of the serenity of the radiant horizons and the loftiness of the sky. So, it was summer... Ah! My pen shouldn't be writing it all down... it was warm, I went out, nobody at home noticed me leaving; there were few people in the streets, the cobblestones were dry, from time to time gusts of hot air would blow up from underground and rise to your head, the walls of the houses reflected the dazzling gleam, and the shade seemed even more burning hot than the light. At the street corners, near the piles of rubbish, swarms of flies were buzzing in the sun's rays, turning slowly like a great golden wheel; the corners of the roofs stood out in sharp straight lines against the blue of the sky, the stones were black, and there were no birds flying round the church steeples.

I walked on, looking for a place to rest, longing for a breeze, something that could sweep me from the surface of the earth and carry me away in a whirlwind.

I left the suburbs, and found myself behind some gardens, in paths that were half streets and half country lanes; here and there, dazzling light pierced through the leaves on the trees, and in the massed shadows blades of grass stood erect, the sharp edges of the pebbles reflected the sun's rays, the dust crackled under my feet, the whole of nature clamped hotly down, and then the sun was hidden; a big cloud came into sight, as if a storm were brewing; the feeling that had been tormenting me up until then changed its character, I was no longer so edgy, but claustrophobic instead; I no longer felt torn apart, but stifled.

I lay down flat on my belly, in the spot where I thought I would have the maximum shade, silence and darkness, the spot that would best conceal me, and, panting, I let my heart wallow in unbridled desire. The clouds were swollen with softness; they weighed down on me and crushed me like one chest on another; I felt a need for pleasure, more heavily laden with perfumes than the scent of the clematis flowers and more scorching than the sun on the garden walls. Ah, if only I could have something to clasp in my arms, to suffocate under my heat, or if only I could make myself double, love that other being and melt into one with it. It was no longer the desire for some vague ideal nor the voluptuous recollection of a lovely faded dream, but, as with rivers that have no fixed beds, my passion overflowed on every side in furious ravines, it flooded my heart and made it echo all around with more giddy tumult than torrents coursing down the mountainsides.

I went to the river-bank; I have always loved water and the gentle undulation of the waves chasing one another; it was flowing peacefully along, and the white water lilies trembled in the murmur of the stream, the ripples rising and falling slowly, unfolding and overtaking one another; in the middle, the islands dangled their thickets of greenery in the water, the river-bank seemed to be smiling, and you could hear nothing but the voice of the waters.

In that spot there were a few big trees; the freshness that spread out from the water and the shade filled me with delight, and I felt myself smiling. Just as the Muse who dwells within us, when she listens to harmony, opens her nostrils and breathes in the lovely sounds, a mysterious something expanded within me to draw in the universal joy; I gazed at the clouds which drifted along in the sky, and the greensward of the river-bank gleaming glossy and yellow in the sunlight, as I listened to the sound of the water and the rustle of the treetops, which were stirring even though there was no wind. All alone, both calm and restless at once, I felt myself growing faint with pleasure beneath the weight of nature's love; and love is what I cried out for! My lips trembled and puckered as if I had sensed the breath of another mouth, my hands sought something to caress, and my eyes tried to discover, in the shape of every folding wave, in the outline of the swelling clouds, some shape, some thrill of pleasure, some revelation; desire oozed from my every pore, my heart was tender and filled with a barely contained harmony, and I shook the hair round my head, caressing my face with it, taking pleasure in breathing in its odour; I stretched out on the moss, at the foot of the trees, longing for even greater and more languorous sensations; I longed to be suffocated in roses, broken by kisses – I longed to be the flower shaken by the wind, the river-bank watered by the river, the earth made fecund by the sun.

The grass was smooth to walk on, so I walked on it; every step gave me a new pleasure, and I enjoyed the sensation of the soft greensward against the soles of my feet. In the distance, the meadows were dotted with animals – horses and foals; the horizon echoed to the sound of their neighing and galloping, the open fields rose and fell gently in broad undulations along the hillsides, the river wound its way along, disappearing behind the islands and reappearing between the grasses and the reeds. It was all a fine spectacle, seemingly contented, following its law, its own course; I alone was sick and in agony, filled with desire.

Suddenly I took flight, and returned to the town, dashing over the bridges; I wandered through the streets and squares; women passed by me, many women, walking swiftly along, all marvellously beautiful; never had I looked so directly into so many faces, staring into their shining eyes, or gazing at the easy way they walked along, light-footed as goats; duchesses, leaning out of the blazoned doors of their carriages, seemed to be smiling at me, inviting me to amorous dalliance on silken drapes; from their balconies, ladies in scarves hung out to see me, and gazed down, saying, 'Love us! Love us!' All of them loved me: I could clearly see it in their posture, their eyes, their very immobility. And then, women were everywhere, on all sides of me, I grazed against them, I breathed their perfume, the air was full of their scent; I could see the sweat on a woman's neck between the shawl wrapped round her and the feathers on her hat that swayed in rhythm with her gait; her heel lifted the hem of her dress as she walked along before me. When I walked past her, her gloved hand was fluttering. Neither this woman nor that one, no single woman more than any other: no, all of them, each of them, in the infinite variety of their forms and the specific desire that corresponded to each form; it was no use their being fully clothed, I would decorate them there and then with a magnificent nudity that my eyes devoured; and soon, as I brushed by them, I was able to carry away with me the greatest number of voluptuous ideas, fragrances that fill you with love for everything, glancing touches that arouse you, and shapes that allure.

I knew full well where I was going: to a house in a little street down which I had often walked so as to feel my heart beating faster; it had green shutters, you went up three steps, oh! I knew the scene by heart, I had gazed at it often enough, and taken a detour from my route simply to see those closed windows. Finally, after what seemed like a century, I came to the street, and thought I was going to suffocate; nobody passed by, and I made my way further and further along; I can still feel the contact of the door that I pushed open with my shoulder; it yielded – I'd been afraid it might be locked, but no, it turned on its hinge, gently, noiselessly.

I made my way up the stairs; the stairwell was dark and the steps worn down and wobbly under my tread; I carried on upwards, unable to see, feeling dazed; no one spoke a word to me, I could hardly breathe. Finally I came into a room, it seemed a big room, but this was due to the darkness; the windows were open, but big yellow curtains, hanging to the ground, kept out the daylight, and the apartment was suffused with a wan golden hue; at the far end, next to the window on the right, a woman was sitting. She couldn't have heard me, since she didn't turn round when I went in; I stood there motionless, gazing at her.

She was wearing a white dress with short sleeves, and sitting with her elbow propped on the window ledge, one hand near her mouth, apparently looking down at something vague and indistinct on the ground; her black hair, smoothed and plaited at the temples, shone like a crow's wings, her head was leaning forward slightly, some wisps of hair at the back stood out from the others and fell in light curls on her neck, and the curve of her big golden comb was crowned with points of red coral.

She uttered a cry when she noticed me and jumped to her feet. I was immediately struck by the shining gaze of her two big eyes; when I was able to look up again and withstand the intensity of that gaze, I saw a face of adorable beauty: a single straight line started from the summit of her head and along the parting in her hair, passed between her two arched eyebrows, down her aquiline nose with its tremulous nostrils flaring like those in ancient cameos, and drew a line down the middle of her warm lip, shadowed by a bluish down... and then came her neck, her plump, white, round neck; through her thin clothes I could see the shape of her breasts rising and falling in rhythm with her breathing; thus she stood before me, framed by the sunlight that passed through the yellow curtains and brought out even more strongly her white clothes and dark head.

Eventually she started to smile, almost out of pity and gentleness, and I walked over. I don't know what she had put on her hair, but it was strongly perfumed, and I felt my heart growing softer and more yielding than a peach melting on my tongue. She said, 'What's the matter with you? Come over here!'

And she went to sit on a long sofa covered with grey canvas, standing against the wall; I sat next to her, she took my hand – hers was warm – and we sat there for a long time gazing at one another wordlessly.

Never had I seen a woman from so close; her beauty was all around me, her arm was touching mine, the folds of her dress fell onto my legs, the heat of her hip set me on fire, and through its contact I could feel the undulations of her body; I gazed at the roundness of her shoulder and the blue veins of her temples. She said to me, 'Well?'

'Well,' I repeated cheerfully, trying to shake off this mesmerising fascination.

But then I stopped, totally intent on devouring her with my eyes. Without speaking, she put her arm round me and drew me towards her, in a silent embrace. Then I took her in my arms and planted my mouth on her shoulder, and ecstatically drank in my first kiss of love, savouring the prolonged desires of my youth and the pleasures of my dreams that had at last come true; and then I flung back my head to see her face more clearly; her eyes were shining, inflaming me, her gaze enveloped me more than her arms, I was lost within her eyes, and our fingers mingled; hers were long and delicate, and turned within my hand in quick, subtle movements; I could have crushed them with the slightest effort, and I squeezed them deliberately so as to feel them more intensely.

I have forgotten what she said to me and what I replied; I sat there for a long time, lost, in suspense, swaying on the beating of my heart; each minute increased my intoxication, at every moment some new impression entered my soul, my whole body was quivering with impatience, desire and joy; and yet I was serious, sombre rather than light-hearted, serious and absorbed as if in something divine, something supreme. With her hand she drew my head against her heart, but gently, as if she had been afraid of crushing me against her.

She removed her sleeve with a twist of her shoulders, and her dress came undone; she had no corset, and her chemise was open. She had splendid breasts, the kind that make you long to die between them, smothered by love. Sitting on my knees, she had the naive pose of a dreaming child; her lovely profile stood out in pure lines; an adorable fold of skin in her armpit seemed like a smile of her shoulder; her white back bent slightly and wearily, and her dress as it fell gathered in broad folds on the floor; she raised her eyes skywards and murmured between her teeth a sad, languorous refrain.

I touched her comb and took it out; her hair came flooding down like a wave, and her long black tresses quivered as they fell to her hips. I immediately ran my hand over it, and in it, and beneath it; I plunged my arm into it, and bathed my face in it, filled with sadness. Sometimes I would enjoy separating it into two, from behind, and then bringing it over her shoulder so as to hide her breasts; then I would bring all her hair together in a mesh, and pull it so that her head came back and her neck was thrown forward; she let me do what I wanted, like a dead woman.

Suddenly she broke away from me, stepped out of her dress, and leapt onto the bed with the litheness of a cat; the mattress sank under the weight of her feet, the bed creaked, she quickly drew back the curtains and lay down, she held out her arms to me and took me in them. Oh! the sheets themselves seemed to be still warm from all the caresses of love that had passed through them.

Her soft damp hand moved over my body, and she kissed me on the face, on the mouth, on the eyes, and each of her urgent caresses made me swoon; she lay on her back and sighed; sometimes she would half close her eyes and look at me with a voluptuous irony, then, propped on one shoulder, she would twist round onto her stomach, raising her heels into the air. She was full of charming little amorous tricks, and refined and innocent movements; finally, abandoning herself impulsively to me, she raised her eyes and heaved a great sigh which lifted her whole body… Her warm skin, all tremulous, stretched out beneath me and shuddered; from my head to my feet I felt a thrill of intense pleasure; my mouth was glued to hers, our fingers were intertwined, quivering in the same rhythm, clasped in the same embrace; and, breathing the odour of her hair and the breath of her lips, I felt myself ecstatically expiring. For a while longer I stayed there, panting, savouring the beating of my heart and the final juddering of my excited nerves; then it seemed as if everything was fading away and disappearing.

But she, too, said nothing; immobile like a statue of flesh, with her abundant black hair round her pale face, and her arms wide open and softly resting; from time to time, a convulsive movement would shake her knees and hips; on her breast, the place where I had kissed her was still red, and a raucous, pitiful sound emerged from her throat, as when someone is going to sleep after a long time weeping and sobbing. Suddenly I heard her saying these words: 'Just imagine if you were swept away by your senses and ended up becoming a mother' – and then I don't remember what happened next, she crossed her legs and rocked from side to side as if she had been in a hammock.

She ran her hand through my hair, teasingly, as if I were a child, and asked me whether I had ever had a mistress; I answered yes, and, as she was about to carry on, I added that she was beautiful and married. She asked me some more questions about my name, my life, and my family.

'And what about you,' I asked her, 'have you ever been in love?'

'In love? No!'

And she burst out into an exaggerated laugh that quite unsettled me.

45

She asked me again if my mistress was beautiful, and after a silence she continued:

'Oh, how she must love you! Tell me your name, go on! Your name!'

I in turn wished to know hers.

'Marie,' she replied. 'But I had another name, that's not what I was called at home.'

And then… well, I don't remember, it's all gone now; it was all such a long time ago! And yet there are certain things that I can still see as clearly as if it were yesterday – her room, for example; I can see the bedspread, threadbare in the middle, the mahogany bed with its ornaments in copper and curtains of red moiré silk; they rustled stiffly if you touched them, and their fringes were faded and worn. On the mantelpiece were two vases of artificial flowers; in the middle, the clock, whose face was suspended between four alabaster columns. Here and there, hanging on the wall, was some old engraving with a black wooden frame, depicting women bathing, harvesters or fishermen.

And as for *her*!… Sometimes a memory of her returns to me, so vivid, so precise, that every detail on her face appears to me again, with that astonishingly faithful memory that dreams alone give us, when we meet again, wearing the same clothes and speaking in the same tone of voice, old friends who have been dead for years – something which fills us with dread. I clearly remember that on her lower lip, on the left side, she had a beauty spot that showed up in a crease when she smiled; indeed, she was no longer in her first youth, and the corner of her mouth was pinched in a bitter and weary fashion.

When I was ready to go, she said goodbye.

'Goodbye!' I replied.

'Shall we be seeing you again?'

'Maybe.'

And I went out; the fresh air gave me new vigour, I found myself quite changed, I imagined that people should be able to see from my face that I was no longer the same man; I walked as if on air, bold, happy and free; I had nothing else to learn, nothing to feel, nothing to desire in life. I returned home, an eternity had gone by since I had left; I went up to my room and sat on my bed, overcome by the events of my long day, which weighed down so incredibly heavily on me. It was perhaps seven o'clock in the evening, the sun was setting, the sky was aflame, and the fiery horizon gleamed red right across the house tops; the garden, already in shade, was filled with melancholy, yellow and orange circles were turning in the corners of the walls, rising and falling in the bushes, the earth was dry and grey; and in the street a few workers, arm in arm with their wives, were singing as they strolled by on their way to the town gates.

I continued to mull over what I had done, and I was overwhelmed by an indefinable sense of sadness, filled with distaste; I was sated and weary. 'But this morning,' I told myself, 'it wasn't like that, I was fresher and happier – why?' And in my mind I went through all the streets I had walked along, I saw again the women I had met, all the paths down which I had wandered; I went back to Marie and dwelt on every detail I could recollect; I squeezed my memory to extract as much as it would yield. I spent the entire evening engaged in this activity; night fell and there I still was, clinging to this delightful thought, like an old man, but sensing that I would never be able to grasp it again, that other loves might come along, but that they would never resemble this one; this first perfume had been savoured, these sounds had faded; I desired my desire and I longed to have my joy back again.

When I considered my former life and my present life – the expectation of former days and the lassitude by which I was now overwhelmed – then I could not tell in which nook of my existence my heart had hidden itself, whether I was dreaming or really acting, whether I were filled with disgust or with desire, since I was experiencing both the nausea of repletion and the ardour of new hope.

So that was all love was! That was all a woman was! Good Lord, why do we still hunger even when we are sated? Why so many aspirations and so many disappointments? Why is man's heart so big and life so small? There are days when even the love of the angels would not suffice it, and in a single hour it grows weary of all the caresses of earth.

But a vanished illusion leaves its fragrance within us, like a fairy, and we seek her trace along every path down which she has fled; we indulge ourselves in the thought that it cannot all be over so soon, that life has only just begun, that a whole world is opening up before us. And indeed, can we have lavished so many sublime dreams and so many seething desires merely to have ended up *here*? I was quite unwilling to give up all the lovely visions I had concocted for myself; I had created for myself, well before my lost virginity, other, vaguer but more beautiful shapes, other pleasures that were, like the desire I had for them, less precise, but heavenly and infinite. The imaginary scenes I had once dreamt up, and that I was now trying to summon back into being, were mixed with the intense memory of my latest sensations, and as the whole combination melded together, phantom and body, dream and reality, the woman I had just left took on for me a synthetic status, in which everything past was summed up and from which everything sprang forth towards the future. Alone, and thinking about her, I continued to turn her this way and that, trying to discover something new in her, something I had not noticed, something that had remained unexplored the first time; the longing to see her again flooded through me, obsessively, like a destiny luring me on, a slope down which I was slipping.

Oh, what a lovely night it was! It was warm, I arrived at her door bathed in sweat, there was a light on in her window; she must be still be awake; I stopped, feeling fearful; I stood there for a long time, not knowing what to do, filled with countless confused anxieties. Once again I went in, and my hand for a second time felt its way up the banister of her staircase and turned the key in her lock.

She was alone, as she had been that morning; she was sitting in the same place, almost in the same posture, but she had changed her dress; this one was black, and the lace trimming round the neck quivered with a life of its own on her white breast; her flesh was glowing, and her face had that lascivious pallor that the flicker of candlelight creates; her mouth half-opened, her hair hanging in curls around her shoulders, and her eyes raised to the sky, she seemed to be seeking some vanished star.

Straight away, she leapt joyfully up, dashed over to me and clasped me in her arms. For us it was one of those shuddering embraces that lovers at night must enjoy when they meet – when, after hours spent straining to see through the darkness, watchfully aware of every crunching of leaves underfoot, every vague shape passing through the clearing, they finally come together and fall into each other's arms.

In a tone of voice that was simultaneously urgent and gentle, she said to me:

'Ah, so you love me! You must, if you have come back to see me! Tell me, oh tell me, sweetheart; do you love me?'

Her words had a high-pitched but melodious sound, like the higher notes played on a flute.

Half falling to her knees and clutching me in her arms, she gazed at me in sombre ecstasy; as for myself, however astonished I was at this sudden onset of passion, I was charmed by it, and filled with pride.

Her satin dress rustled under my fingers as if emitting sparks; then, after feeling how velvety soft the fabric was, I came to the warm softness of her bare arm, and her clothes seemed to be alive and sharing in her intimate being, breathing with the allure of the most luxuriant nudity.

She wanted at all costs to sit on my knees, and she started to caress me in her usual fashion, running her hand through my hair while she gazed fixedly at me, face to face, her eyes probing mine. In this immobile pose, her pupils seemed to dilate, and from them flowed a fluid that I felt flooding down into my heart; each wave of that wide-eyed gaze, like the successive circles described by a sea eagle, put me in deeper and deeper thrall to that terrible magic.

'Ah, so you love me!' she resumed, 'you must love me since you've come back to see me again, you've come back for me! But what's the matter? You're not saying anything, you're all sad! Don't you want me any more?'

She paused and then continued:

'How lovely you are, my angel! As lovely as the daylight! So hold me tight, love me! A kiss, quick, a kiss!'

She hung on my mouth and, cooing like a dove, her breast swelled with a deep sigh.

'Ah, but stay for the night, yes, for the night, the whole night, the two of us! It's someone like you that I'd like to have as a lover, a fresh young lover, who would love me dearly, who would think only of me. Oh, how I would love him!'

And she drew in her breath in that deeply passionate way that seems to summon God from the heavens.

'But don't you have one?' I asked her.

'Who? Me? Are *we* poor women ever loved? Does anyone ever think of us? Who would have us? Even you – will you even remember me tomorrow? Perhaps you'll merely say, "Hm, well yesterday I slept with a whore," but brrr! Oh la la!' (and she started to dance, her hands on her hips, with lascivious gestures). 'I do dance well! Just look at my costume.'

She opened her cupboard, and I saw on a shelf a black mask and some blue ribbons with a domino; there was also a pair of black velvet trousers with gold braid, hanging from a nail – the faded remnants of the last carnival.

'My poor costume,' she said, 'how often I went to the ball with it! I was the one dancing this winter!'

The window was open and the candle was flickering in the wind; she took it off the mantelpiece and placed it on her night table. She sat on the bed and fell into a deep musing, her head lowered on her breast. I too was silent, waiting; the warm odours of an August night rose up to us, and we could hear, from where we were, the rustle of the trees on the boulevard, and the curtain swaying at the window; all night long a storm raged; often, in the flashes of lightning, I caught sight of her wan face, twisted in an expression of passionate sadness; the clouds scudded across the sky, the moon, half hidden behind them, shone out from time to time in a patch of clear sky surrounded by dark clouds.

She undressed slowly, with the regular movements of a machine. When she was in her chemise, she came towards me, barefoot across the floor, took me by the hand and led me to her bed; she was not looking at me, but thinking of something else; her lips were pink and damp, her nostrils flaring, her eyes fiery, and she seemed to be vibrating in tune with her thoughts just as, even when the artist is no longer there, the melodious instrument gives off a secret fragrance of slumbering notes.

It was when she was lying next to me that she displayed for me, with a courtesan's pride, all the splendours of her flesh. I saw her breast naked and firm, constantly swelling as with a tempestuous murmur, her belly of pearl, with its deep navel, her belly, supple and convulsive, as soft for your head to plunge into as a pillow of warm silk; she had superb hips, real womanly hips, the lines of which, as they curve down onto a round thigh, always remind me in profile of some supple and corrupt shape of a snake or a demon; the sweat beading her skin made it fresh and clinging, in the darkness her eyes shone with alarming intensity, and the amber bracelet she wore on her right arm rang out when she dashed it against the wainscoting of the alcove. It was during those hours that she said to me, holding my head tightly to her breast:

'My angel of love, delight, and pleasure, where do you come from? Where is your mother? What was she thinking of when she conceived you? Was she dreaming of the strength of African lions or the perfume of those distant trees, so powerful that you die if you smell them? You're not speaking; look at me with your big eyes, look at me, look at me! Your mouth! Your mouth! Look now – here is mine!'

And then her teeth would start chattering as if in some intense cold, and her parted lips trembled and uttered crazy words into the air:

'Ah, I would be jealous of you, you know, if we loved one another; the least woman who looked at you...'

And she completed her phrase with a cry. At other times she would stop me with taut, outstretched arms, telling me in a low voice that she was going to die.

'Oh, how handsome he is, a man when he is young! If *I* were a man, all women would love me, my eyes would gleam so brightly! I would be so elegantly dressed, so attractive! Your mistress loves you, doesn't she? I'd like to make her acquaintance. How do you manage to see each other? Is it in your house or hers? Is it when you go out riding? You must look so good on a horse! Or in the theatre, when people are leaving and her coat is handed to her? Or at night in her garden? Ah what hours of rapture you pass, I imagine, talking together, sitting under the bower!'

I let her have her say – it struck me that with these words she was fabricating an ideal mistress for me, and I loved this phantom who had just come into my mind and was shining with a gleam as transient as that of a will-o'-the-wisp, on country evenings.

'Have you known each other for long? Tell me about it. What do you say to make her happy? Is she tall or petite? Can she sing?'

I could not hold back from telling her that she was mistaken, and I even told her of my apprehensiveness in coming to see her – of my remorse, or rather of the strange fear that had subsequently seized me, and then the sudden renewed longing that had driven me back to her. When I had explained to her that I didn't have a mistress, that I'd been looking for one everywhere, that I'd dreamt for ages of having one, and that she in fact was the first woman who had tolerated my caresses, she drew closer, filled with astonishment, and seizing my arm, as if I were some illusion she wanted to grasp, she said:

'Is that true? Oh, don't lie to me! So you're a virgin, and I was the one to deflower you, my poor angel? Yes, your kisses did have something naive about them, they were like ones that only children would give, if they ever made love. But you surprise me! You are charming; the more I look at you, the more I love you; your cheeks are as soft as peaches, and your skin is white all over; you have lovely hair, strong and abundant. Ah, how much I'd love you, if you wanted! I've never seen anyone quite like you; you seem to gaze on me with kindness, and yet your eyes burn into me; I always have this longing to get close to you and to clasp you to me.'

These were the first words of love I had ever heard in my life. Wherever such words come from, our hearts accept them with a shudder of bliss. Just remember this! I drank them in with delight. Oh, how swiftly I soared aloft into this new sky!

'Yes, yes, kiss me, kiss me do! Your kisses rejuvenate me,' she repeated. 'I love the smell of you, it's like that of my honeysuckle in June, fresh and sweet at the same time; your teeth – show me! – are whiter than mine, I'm no longer as good-looking as you are… Ah, how nice this spot is, just here!'

And she fastened her mouth to my neck, burrowing into it with fierce kisses, like a wild beast into its victim's belly.

'What can be wrong with me, this evening? You've set me completely on fire, I feel like drinking, and singing and dancing. Have you ever wanted to be a little bird? We would fly off together, it must be delightful to make love in the air, the winds blow you along, and clouds surround you… No, be quiet, just let me look at you, look at you for a long time, so I will always be able to remember you!'

'Whatever for?'

'Whatever for?' she echoed. 'But… to remember you, to think of you; I'll think of you at night when I can't sleep, and in the morning, when I wake up, I'll think of you all day long, leaning on my window watching the passers-by; but especially in the evening, when I can't see anything and still haven't lit my candles; I'll remember your face, your body, your lovely body, aglow with pleasure, and your voice! Oh! Listen, I beg you, my love, let me cut off a lock of your hair, I'll set it in that bracelet, there – it will never leave me.'

She immediately rose to her feet, went to fetch her scissors and cut off a lock of hair from the back of my head. They were small pointed scissors that squeaked on their screw; I can still feel on the nape of my neck the cold steel and the hand of Marie.

A lock of hair given and exchanged is one of the finest of lovers' trophies. How many pretty hands, from time immemorial, have slipped through balconies at night to present a gift of black tresses! Down with those figure-of-eight watch chains, those rings onto which they are glued, the medallions on which they are arranged in trefoil, and all those locks that have been polluted by the commonplace hand of a hairdresser! I want them to be simple and tied together by a thread at each end, for fear of losing a single strand; you have cut them yourself from the beloved head, in some sublime moment, at the height of a first love affair or on the eve of a separation. A head of hair! In primal days, the hair formed a woman's magnificent mantle, when it fell to her heels and covered her arms, when she would walk along with man along the banks of great rivers, and the first breezes of creation blew simultaneously through the tops of palm trees, the manes of lions, and the hair of women! I love hair. How often, in the cemeteries where gravediggers were turning over the soil, or in old churches that were being demolished, have I gazed on hair that appeared in the broken earth, between the yellow bones and fragments of rotten wood! Often the sun would shed on it a wan ray, making it gleam like a seam of gold; I loved to dream of the days when this hair had been gathered together on a white scalp and anointed with liquid perfumes, and some hand, now withered, had stroked it and spread it out on the pillow, or some mouth, its gums now shrivelled away, had kissed it in the middle and grazed on its strands, sobbing with happiness.

I allowed her to cut my hair, filled with a foolish vanity, and shamefully I did not ask for hers in return; now, when I have nothing – not a glove, not a belt, not even three corollas of rose dried and kept within a book, nothing but a memory of the love of a common whore – I regret it.

When she had finished, she came and curled up next to me again, slipping between the sheets with a quiver of pleasure; she was shivering, and huddled up to me like a child; eventually she went to sleep, leaving her head cradled on my chest.

Each time I drew breath, I could feel the weight of that sleeping head rising on my heart. In what intimate communion did I thus find myself with this unknown creature? We had been hitherto unaware of each other, but now chance had brought us together, we were there in the same bed, linked together by a nameless force; we were going to separate and never see one another again; the atoms that turn and float through the air have longer encounters than those enjoyed on earth by loving hearts; at night, no doubt, solitary desires arise and dreams start to seek out other dreams, and one person will maybe yearn for the unknown soul that yearns for it in turn in another hemisphere, beneath other skies.

What were the dreams that, now, were passing through *this* head? Was she dreaming of her family, of her first lover, of society, of men, of some rich life glittering with opulence, of some longed-for love? Of me, perhaps! My eye fixed on her pale forehead, I watched attentively over her sleep, and tried to discover a meaning in the strident noise emerging from her nostrils.

It was raining; I listened to the rain falling and Marie sleeping; the lights, about to go out, sputtered in the glass sconces. The day dawned, and a yellow line rose swiftly into the sky, lengthened horizontally and, assuming ever more golden, ruby hues, filled the apartment with a faint wan light, with a pale purple sheen, which continued to tussle playfully with the night and the gleam of the dying candles, reflected in the window.

Marie, lying across me, thus had some parts of her body in the light, and others in the shade; she had changed position a little, her head was lower than her breasts; her right arm, the arm with her bracelet on, was hanging out of the bed and almost touching the floor; on the night table was a bouquet of violets in a vase of water; I reached out and took it, breaking the thread with my teeth and breathing in the odour. The heat of the day before, perhaps, or the long time that had passed since they were gathered, had withered them; I found they had an exquisite and quite particular scent, and I breathed in the fragrance of each flower one by one; as they were dripping with water, I applied them to my eyes to cool myself down, since my blood was on fire, and my weary limbs felt as if they burnt on contact with the sheets. Then, not knowing what to do and not wishing to awaken her, since I took a strange pleasure in seeing her sleeping, I gently placed all the violets on Marie's breast; she was soon covered all over by them, and those lovely withered flowers, under which she lay sleeping, symbolised her in my mind. And like those flowers, in spite of their vanished freshness, or perhaps because of it, she wafted towards me a sharper and more acrid odour; misfortune, which must have passed through her life, made her beautiful with the bitterness that her mouth preserved, even as she slept, beautiful with the two wrinkles at the back of her neck which in the daytime she no doubt concealed beneath her hair. Seeing this woman, so melancholy in pleasure, whose embraces themselves had a lugubrious joy to them, I guessed at the countless terrible passions that must have left their furrows on her like a thunderbolt, to judge from the remaining traces; what a pleasure it would have been to hear her relate her life to me, as I was seeking all that was resounding and vibrant in human existence, the world of great passions and lovely tears.

Just then she awoke, all the violets fell from her, and she smiled, her eyes still half-closed; at the same time, she stretched her arms round my neck and embraced me with a long morning kiss, the kiss of an awakening dove.

When I asked her to tell me her story, she said:

'Yes, I can tell it to you. Other women would lie and would begin by telling you that they haven't always been what they are now; they'd tell you fairy stories about their families and their love affairs, but I don't want to deceive you or pass myself off as a princess; listen, you'll see whether I was happy! Do you know I've often felt like killing myself? Once they reached my room when I was already half asphyxiated. Oh, if I weren't afraid of hell, it would have been all over long ago. I'm afraid of dying, too, it frightens me to think I have to go through that, and yet I long to be dead!

'I come from the countryside, our father was a farmer. Until my first communion, they used to send me out every morning to look after the cows in the fields; all day long I stayed there by myself, sitting on the edge of a ditch and going to sleep, or else I went into the wood to go bird's-nesting; I could climb trees like a boy, and my clothes were always torn; I often got a beating for stealing apples, or allowing the animals to wander into the neighbours' fields. When it was harvest, we'd all dance in a ring in the farmyards at evening time, and I heard songs being sung in which there were things I didn't understand; the boys would kiss the girls, there'd be gales of laughter; this made me sad and dreamy. Sometimes, on the road home, I would ask if I could get up into a hay wagon; the man would take me with him, telling me to sit on the bales of alfalfa. Would you believe it? I eventually felt an inexpressible pleasure feeling myself being lifted up off the ground by the strong, robust hands of a vigorous fellow whose face was burnt by the sun and whose chest was streaming with sweat. Usually his sleeves were rolled right up to his armpits; I liked to touch his muscles that made bumps and hollows with each movement of his hand, and I enjoyed being embraced by him, and feeling his beard rasping against my cheek. At the bottom of the meadow where I went every day there was a narrow stream between two rows of poplars, along which all kinds of flowers grew; I would weave bouquets, wreaths and chains of them; with the seeds of sorb trees I would make necklaces for myself; this became an obsession, my apron was always full of them, so that my father would scold me, telling me I would never be anything but a coquette. I'd put some in my little bedroom, too; sometimes all these many odours intoxicated me, and I would doze off, my head heavy, but revelling in this sickly sensation. The odour of mown hay, for example, of warm fermented hay, has always struck me as quite delicious; as a result, on Sundays, I would shut myself away in the barn, spending my entire afternoon watching the spiders spinning their webs in the lintels, and listening to the flies buzzing. I lived like a lazy girl, but I was growing into a fine lass all the same, strong and healthy. Often I would be seized by a kind of madness, and I would start running and running until I dropped, or else I would sing at the top of my voice, or talk to myself for ages; strange desires possessed me, I constantly gazed at the pigeons, there in their dovecote, making love to one another – some of them would come right up beneath my window to frolic in the sunshine and play around in the vine branches. At night, I could still hear the beating of their wings, and their cooings which seemed so soft and gentle that I would have liked to be a pigeon like them, and twist and turn my neck in the same way that they did when they embraced. "What can they be saying to each other," I thought, "that makes them seem so happy?" And I also remembered the proud gallop of the steeds chasing the mares, and how their nostrils flared wide open; I remembered the joy with which the wool on the ewe's back would quiver at the approach of the ram, and the murmur of the bees when they hung in clusters from the trees in the orchard. I would often slip between the animals in the cowshed to smell the odour given off by their limbs, the steam of life that I breathed in with full lungs; and I would furtively contemplate their nudity, to which a dizzy longing always attracted my troubled eyes. At other times, at the edge of a wood, especially at dusk, the trees themselves would assume strange shapes: sometimes they were arms rising heavenwards, or else the trunk would twist and turn like a body being bent by the wind. At night, when I woke up and the moon and the stars were out, I would see in the sky things that filled me simultaneously with dread and longing. I remember that once, one Christmas Eve, I saw a great naked woman, standing erect, with rolling eyes; she must have been a hundred feet high, but along she drifted, growing ever longer and ever thinner, and finally fell apart, each limb remaining separate, with the head floating away first as the rest of her body continued to waver. Or else I would dream; already at the age of ten I had feverish nights, nights filled with lust. Wasn't it lust that shone in my eyes, coursed through my blood, and made my heart leap whenever my limbs grazed against each other? It was lust that sang into my ear never-ending canticles of pleasure; in my visions, flesh shone like gold, and unknown shapes ran here and there, like spilt quicksilver.

'In church I would gaze at the man spread naked on the cross, and I would lift up his head, fill in the wounds in his side, colour all his limbs, and open his eyes for him; I would fabricate an alluring man for myself, one with a burning gaze; I would detach him from the cross and bring him down to me, on the altar, where he was swathed in incense; he would come towards me through the smoke, and my skin would prickle with a sensual shudder.

'Whenever a man spoke to me, I would examine his eye and the beam darting from it; I especially liked the men whose eyelids are always moving, showing the whites of their eyes and then hiding them, fluttering like the wing beat of a moth; through their clothes I tried to sense the secrets of their sex, and I would ask my girlfriends for information about this topic; I would spy on the kisses exchanged between my father and mother, and at night I listened to the noises they made in bed.

'At the age of twelve I made my first communion; a lovely white dress was ordered and sent to me from town, and we all had blue belts; I would have liked them to arrange my hair in curl papers, like a lady. Before setting off to church, I gazed at myself in the mirror; I was as pretty as a cherub, and almost fell in love with myself – I wished I really could! It was about the time of Corpus Christi; the nuns had filled the church with flowers and fragrances; I too had been working with the others for three days, decking with jasmine the little table on which you make your vows. The altar was covered with hyacinths, the chancel steps covered with carpets; we were all wearing white gloves and holding candles; I was filled with happiness, I felt I was made for this ceremony; throughout the mass, my feet caressed the carpet, since there wasn't one in my father's house; I longed to lie down on it, in my lovely dress, and stay there all alone in the church, in the midst of the gleaming candles; my heart was beating with a new hope, I awaited the host with anxiety, having heard that first communion changed your life, and I thought that, after taking the sacrament, I would find that all my desires calmed down. Far from it! Returning to my seat, I found I was still in my furnace; I'd noticed people looking at me as I went up to the priest, admiring me; I strutted, reflected how beautiful I was, and took an undefined pride in all the delights hidden within me, of which I was as yet unaware.

'On coming out of the mass, we all processed in a line, through the cemetery; the parents and idle onlookers were standing on either side in the grass, watching us go by; I walked at the head of the others, being the biggest. During the dinner I ate nothing, my heart felt heavy and oppressed; my mother, who had wept during the service, was still red-eyed; some of our neighbours came over to congratulate me and effusively hugged me, but their embrace filled me with revulsion. In the evening, at vespers, there were even more people than there had been in the morning. Opposite us, the boys were seated; they gazed at us avidly, especially at me; even when I kept my eyes lowered, I could still sense their gaze. Their hair had been curled, and they were all dressed up, like us. When we had sung the first two lines of a canticle, they would continue with the next two, and their voices made my soul soar; and when they faded away, my rapture would die too, only to take new flight when they resumed. I made my vows; the only thing I remember about them is that I spoke of a white dress and of innocence.'

Marie paused here, no doubt absorbed in the touching memory which she feared might overwhelm her; then she continued, with a despairing laugh:

'Ah, the white dress! It's been threadbare for a long time! And innocence with it! Where are the other girls now? Some are dead, others are married with children; I don't see any of them any more, I don't know anyone. Every New Year's Day, I still want to write to my mother, but I daren't, and anyway – who cares, all those feelings are plain silly!'

She struggled to master her emotion, and then continued:

'The next day, which was another holiday, a friend came to play with me. My mother said, "Now you're a big girl, you shouldn't go around with boys any more," and she separated us. That was all I needed to make me fall in love with the boy in question; I sought him out and courted him, I longed to run away from home with him, he was going to marry me when I was old enough, I called him my husband, my lover... but he didn't dare. One day we were alone, coming back together from the wood where we'd gone to pick strawberries; we were passing by a hayrick when I jumped on him, covering him with my whole body and kissing him on the mouth; I started to shout, "Go on, love me, let's get married, let's get married!" He pulled away from under me and ran off.

'From that time on, I shunned society and no longer left the farm; I lived all alone in my desires, as others do in their pleasures. If I heard people talking about such-and-such a lad who'd made off with a girl they had refused to let him have, I imagined being his mistress, fleeing with him on the back of his horse, across the fields, holding him tight in my arms;

if there was talk of a wedding, I would quickly lie down in the white bed, and just like the new bride I would tremble with fear and pleasure; I even envied the plaintive lowing of the cattle when they are calving; dreaming of the cause, I was jealous of their pain.

'At that time my father died, and my mother took me to the town with her; my brother left to join the army, where he has since become a captain. I was sixteen when we left the house.

'I said a last farewell to the woods, and the meadow with my stream; farewell to the porch of the church, where I had spent such happy hours playing in the sunshine, and farewell to my poor little bedroom; I've never seen any of those things since. Some of the local ladies of easy virtue became my friends and showed me their lovers; I'd go to parties with them, see how they loved each other, and drink in the spectacle at my leisure. Every day I found some new pretext for taking off; my mother noticed and at first she was cross, but in the end she left me alone.

'Finally, one day, an old woman whom I had known for a while proposed that I make my fortune, telling me she had found a really wealthy lover for me. All I needed to do was to go out as if I were delivering work to some address in a different part of town, and she'd take me there.

'Over the following twenty-four hours, I kept thinking I would go mad; as the hour approached, the time arranged grew more distant; the only word in my head was "a lover! a lover!" – I was going to have a lover, I was going to be loved, so I was going to love! I first put on my slenderest shoes, then, seeing that my feet seemed splayed in them, I took some ankle boots; in addition, I arranged my hair in a hundred different ways – in coils, then parted down the middle, then in curl papers, then in plaits; the more I gazed at myself in the mirror, the more beautiful I seemed, but I still wasn't beautiful enough, my clothes were perfectly ordinary, and I blushed with shame. Why wasn't I one of those women all white in their velvet, abundantly decked out with lace, giving off an odour of amber and rose, with a rustle of silk, and servants covered from head to foot in gold braid! I cursed my mother, my past life, and I fled, driven by all the devil's temptations, and savouring them all in advance.

'At a street corner a fiacre was waiting for us, and we climbed into it; an hour later, it dropped us off at the gate of a country park. We wandered about there for a while, and then I realised that the old woman had left, and I continued walking along the broad alleys alone. The trees were tall, covered all over with leaves, and wide strips of lawn surrounded the flower-beds; I had never seen such a beautiful garden – there was a river flowing through the middle, and stones artfully arranged here and there formed little waterfalls; swans were playing on the water and, with swelling wings, allowed themselves to drift with the current. I also took pleasure at the aviary, where birds of every kind were chirruping and swinging on their rings; they displayed their gaudy tail feathers and strutted in front of one another; it was a dazzling sight. Two statues of white marble, at the foot of the flight of steps, gazed at one another in charming poses; the great pool opposite gleamed gold in the light of the setting sun and made you long to swim in it. I thought of the unknown lover who lived there; at any moment I expected to see emerging from behind a clump of trees some handsome man striding proudly along like an Apollo. After dinner, when the bustle from the chateau, which had been audible for some time, was finally stilled, my master appeared. He was an old man, pale and skinny, whose clothes were too tight and clung to him; he was wearing the cross of the Legion of Honour on his lapel, and he had trouser-straps that prevented him from bending his knees; he had a big nose, and small green eyes with a malicious gleam in them. He came up to me with a smile; he had lost all his teeth. When a person smiles, he should have little pink lips like yours, with the shadow of a moustache at either side, don't you think, my darling?

'We sat down together on a bench, he took my hands, he thought them so pretty that he kissed each finger in turn; he told me that if I wished to be his mistress, to be a good girl and stay with him, I'd be very rich, I'd have my own servants to look after me, and beautiful dresses every day; I'd go out riding on horses and in carriages; but in return for all that, he said, I had to love him. I promised him that I would love him.

'And yet I now felt none of those burning inner flames that had previously set my belly on fire at the approach of men; simply by sitting next to him and telling myself that this was the man whose mistress I was going to be, I finally started to feel desire. When he told me to go indoors with him, I jumped to my feet; he was delighted, the old chap – trembling with joy! We crossed a splendid salon, where the furniture was all gilded, he led me to my room and tried to undress me himself; he started by taking off my bonnet, but when he then attempted to take off my shoes, he had difficulty in bending down and told me, "I'm an old man, my child"; he was on his knees, gazing imploringly at me; he added, clasping his hands together, "You are so pretty!" – and I was afraid of what was going to follow.

'An enormous bed was set in the alcove, and he pulled me over to it with a cry; I felt as if I were drowning in all the eiderdown and the mattresses, his body weighed down on mine, it was the most dreadful torment, his flabby lips covered mine with cold kisses, the bedroom ceiling was crushing me. How happy he was! He was positively swooning! Trying in turn to feel some excitement, I managed to stimulate his senses, at least so it appeared; but what did I care about his pleasure! It was my pleasure that I needed, it was mine that I longed for, I tried to suck it from his hollow mouth and his feeble limbs, I drew as much as I could from every bit of that old man, and made an incredible effort to combine all the lubricious longings pent up within me, but the only feeling I succeeded in summoning up was a sense of disgust at my first night of debauchery.

'Hardly had he left than I rose and went over to the window; I opened it and let the air cool my skin; I would have liked the ocean to wash me clean of him; I remade my bed, carefully smoothing down all the places where that corpse had laboured me with his convulsions. I spent the whole night weeping; in despair, I moaned aloud like a tiger that has just been castrated. Ah, if only you had turned up just then! If only we had got to know each other at that time! If only you had been the same age as me, then we could have loved one another, when I was sixteen, when my heart was fresh! Our entire lives would have been spent in love, my arms would have worn themselves out in hugging you to me, and my eyes in gazing deep into yours.'

She continued:

'I was now a great lady: I got up at midday, I had liveried servants who followed me everywhere, and a calash in which I could stretch out full length on cushions; my pedigree courser could jump wonderfully well over the tree trunks, and the black plume of my riding hat swayed gracefully; but as I had become rich overnight, all this luxury merely aroused more desires instead of appeasing them. Soon I had a reputation;

men competed to have me; my lovers would do innumerable crazy things to please me; every evening I would read that day's love letters, trying to find the new expression of some heart cast in a different mould from the others and meant for me alone. But they were all alike; I knew in advance how their phrases would end and the way they would fall to their knees; there were two I rejected on a whim, they killed themselves – their deaths didn't affect me; whatever did they have to go and die for? Why didn't they overcome every obstacle to have me? If *I* loved a man, there would not be any sea too vast nor any wall too high that would stop me reaching him. If I had been a man, how easily I would have found a way to bribe guards, to climb up to windows at night-time, and to stifle under my lips the cries of my victim, a victim deceived each morning by the hope I had fostered the night before!

'I drove them away in anger and took others; the monotony of pleasure drove me to distraction, and I ran after it in frenzied pursuit, always athirst for new pleasures that I had magnificently dreamt of; I was like mariners in distress who drink the seawater and cannot stop themselves drinking it, they are so parched by thirst!

'Dandies or boors, I wanted to see if they were all the same; I savoured the passion of men with flabby, white hands, their dyed hair stuck to their temples; I had pale adolescents, as blond and effeminate as girls, who came to expire on me; old men too sullied me with their decrepit joys, and when I awoke I would contemplate their oppressed chests and their lifeless eyes. On a wooden bench, in some village tavern, between a jar of wine and a pipe of tobacco, a man of the people too would seize me in his violent embrace; like him, I put on a display of coarse joy and easy-going manners; but the common rabble don't make love any better than the nobility, and a bale of hay is no warmer than a sofa. To inflame their ardour, I devoted myself to some of them as their slave girl, and they did not love me any the more; for complete dolts I lowered myself to the most degrading level, and in return they hated and despised me, whereas I longed to lavish a hundred times more caresses on them and drown them in happiness. Finally, hoping that people with deformities might love better than the others, and that sickly natures would tend to cling to life by its pleasures, I gave myself to hunchbacks, negroes, dwarves; I gave them nights fit to fill a millionaire with jealousy, but maybe I alarmed them, since they soon left me. Neither rich nor poor, handsome nor ugly managed to assuage the love I begged them to satisfy; all of them, feeble, wilting, conceived in tedium, stunted freaks spawned by paralytics who easily get drunk on wine and are killed by women, fearful of dying between the sheets the way others die in battle – there was not one I didn't see exhausted after just one hour. So there are no longer any of those divine youths left on earth as once there were! No more Bacchuses, no more Apollos, no more of those heroes who strode forth naked, crowned with vine leaves and laurels! *I* was made to be the mistress of an emperor; I needed the love of a bandit, on a stony rock under the African sun; I longed for the embrace of serpents, and the roaring kisses that lions exchange with one another.

'At that time I used to read a great deal; there were two books in particular that I read over and over: *Paul and Virginie* and another one called *The Crimes of Queens*. This included portraits of Messalina, Theodora, Marguerite of Burgundy, Mary Stuart and Catherine II.[4] "Be a queen," I said to myself, "and make the crowd fall in love with you!" Well, I *was* a queen, a queen in the way one can be nowadays; on entering my box in the theatre I would sweep the audience with a triumphant and provocative gaze, the heads of countless people followed every twitch of my eyebrows, and I dominated everything by the insolence of my beauty.

'Still, tired of endlessly having to pursue a lover, and desiring one more than ever, at any price, and having made of vice a cherished source of torment, I rushed to this place, my heart aflame as if my virginity were still for sale; despite my refined tastes, I resigned myself to living in squalor; despite my love of opulence, I was ready to sleep in poverty, since by dint of descending so low, I perhaps no longer aspired to climb ever upwards; as my organs exhausted themselves, my cravings would no doubt slacken; I wished in this way to shed them once and for all, and to lose any taste for what I had once so fervently desired. Yes: though I had bathed in strawberries and milk, I came here to lie down on that dirty mattress which everyone tramples underfoot; instead of being the mistress of one man, I made myself the servant of all – and what a harsh master I thereby took! No more fire in the winter, no more fine wines with my meals, I have worn the same dress for a year – but never mind! Isn't it my job to be naked? But my last thought, my last hope – do you know what it is? Oh, I was counting on it: it was that one day I might find what I had never encountered, the man who has always evaded me, whom I have pursued in the beds of dapper young men and in the dress circles of theatres. He's a fantasy figure who exists only in my heart and whom I long to hold in my hands; one fine day, I hoped, someone is bound to come – there is every probability: someone who is taller, nobler, stronger; he will have wide-open eyes like those of sultan's wives, his voice will utter well-rounded, lascivious melodies, his limbs will have the terrible and voluptuous suppleness of leopards, he will smell of odours so strong that they make you swoon, and his teeth will sink with delight into this swelling breast. At each new arrival

I asked myself, "Is this him?" and at another, "Is it him? Let him love me! Let him love me! Let him beat me! Let him break me! All by myself I will comprise a whole harem for him; I know the flowers that stimulate and the drinks that intoxicate, and how even exhaustion can be transformed into a blissful ecstasy. I will be coquettish when he wants me to be, to irritate his vanity or amuse his mind, and then all at once he will find me soft and yielding like a reed, breathing gentle words and sighs of tenderness; for him I will twist in snaky coils, at night I will quiver in sudden spasms and violent shudders. In some warm country, drinking fine wine from a crystal goblet, I will dance Spanish dances for him, with castanets, or else I will jump into the air shrieking a war chant, like savage women; if he is a lover of statues and paintings, I will drape myself in the poses of the great masters, and before them he will fall to his knees; if he prefers me to be his bosom friend, I will dress as a man, and go hunting with him; I will help him perform his acts of vengeance; if he wishes to assassinate someone, I will be his lookout; if he is a robber, we will commit robberies together; I will love his clothes and the coat in which he is wrapped." But no – never! never! Time may have elapsed and one morning succeeded another; each part of my body has been worn down in vain by every pleasure employed by men for their delectation: I have stayed exactly the way I was, at ten years old – a virgin, if a virgin is a woman who has no husband and no lover, who has never known pleasure and dreams of it ceaselessly, who concocts alluring phantoms for herself and sees them in her dreams, who hears their voices in the sound of the winds, who seeks their features in the face of the moon. I am a virgin! Does that make you laugh? But don't I have the vague presentiments, the ardent yearnings of a virgin? I have everything that belongs to a virgin, except virginity itself.

'Look at my bedhead, where you see all those criss-crossed lines on the mahogany; they are the marks left by the fingernails of all those who have twisted and turned there, all those whose heads have bumped up against it; I never had a thing in common with them; we were united as intimately as human arms can permit, and yet a gulf always separated me from them. Oh, how often, as they were driven wild, and longing to be swallowed up into the depths of their ecstasy, did I mentally take myself off to a place a thousand leagues from there, to share the rush mat of a savage, or the cave, adorned with sheepskins, of some shepherd of the Abruzzi!

'Indeed, no one comes for me, no one knows me; they seek in me, perhaps, a particular woman, just as I seek in them a particular man; in the streets, don't we see more than one dog trotting along sniffing at the piles of rubbish, looking for chicken bones and scraps of meat? In the same way, who will ever know of all the exalted loves that are lavished on a common whore, all the fine elegies contained in the "hello" that is addressed to her? How many men have I seen arriving here, their hearts filled with resentment and their eyes with tears! Some of them have just left a ball and want to find a woman who epitomises all those they have just left behind; others, after getting married, are excited by the idea of innocence; and then there are the young men, eager to caress at their leisure the mistresses to whom they dare not speak, as they close their eyes and see her thus in their hearts; husbands who long to rejuvenate themselves and savour the easy pleasures of the good old days, priests driven by the devil and desiring not so much a woman as a courtesan, sin incarnate; they curse me, they take fright at me and then they adore me. For the temptation to be even greater and the fear more intense, they would like me to have a cloven hoof and my dress to sparkle with jewels. All of them pass along in monotonous and melancholy fashion, like shadows following one after another, like a throng which leaves behind only a faint echo, the fading of its urgent, hurrying footsteps, and the muffled clamour that it raised. And can I remember the name of a single one of them? They come and they go, leaving me behind, with never a disinterested caress – and what caresses they demand! They would demand love, too, if they dared! You have to call them handsome and pretend they are rich: and then they smile. And they love to laugh, sometimes you have to sing for them, or else hold your tongue, or talk to them. In this woman, so familiar to everyone, nobody suspected there was a heart; imbeciles who praised the curve of my eyebrows and the dazzling whiteness of my shoulders, delighted that they could get a king's ransom so cheaply – and never responding to that inextinguishable love that ran out to meet them and threw itself at their feet!

'And yet I do come across women who have lovers, even here – real lovers who love them; these women grant them a place apart, in their beds as in their hearts, and when their lovers come to see them, they are really happy. It is for these men, you see, that they spend such a long time combing their hair and watering the pots of flowers in their window boxes; but for me there is nobody, nobody; not even the peaceful affection of a poor child, since they point her out to him – "that prostitute" – and they pass by her with bowed heads. How long ago it is, my God, since I went out into the fields and saw the countryside! How many Sundays I have spent listening to the sound of those sad bells that summon everyone to the church services – which I never attend! How long it is since I heard the cowbells in the copse! Oh, I want to go away from here, I'm bored, bored; I'll go back home on foot, I'll go and see my nurse, she's a good woman and she'll give me a warm welcome. When I was small, I'd go to her house, where she gave me milk; now I'll help her to raise her children and do the housework, I'll go to fetch kindling wood in the forest, we'll warm ourselves, in the evenings, by the fireside when it snows – winter will soon be here; on Twelfth Night we will pass the cake round to find the bean king. Oh, she'll really love me, I'll lull the children to sleep – how happy I'll be!'

She stopped, and then lifted to me her eyes that were gleaming through her tears, as if to ask me, 'Is it you?'

I had listened to her avidly, I had watched all the words on her lips, trying to identify with the life that they were expressing. Suddenly assuming a stature that, no doubt, I myself endowed her with, she struck me as a new woman, full of unknown mysteries and, in spite of my relationship with her, offering all the temptations of a provocative allure and novel charms. Indeed, the men who had possessed her had left on her, as it were, the whiff of a faded perfume, and the trace of long-gone passions, which gave her a voluptuous majesty; debauchery embellished her with an infernal beauty. Without her past orgies, would she have had that suicidal smile, which made her resemble a dead woman awakening to love? Her cheek was all the paler for it, her hair more supple and perfumed, her limbs more agile, softer and warmer; like me, she had made her way from joy to sorrow, run from hope to bitter disillusionment, and fits of indescribable despondency had succeeded spasms of frenzy; without knowing each other, we had followed the same path, she in her prostitution and I in my chastity – and this path had led to the same abyss; while I had been looking for a mistress, she had been looking for a lover, she in society, and I within my heart, and the objects of our desire had evaded us both.

'Poor woman,' I said to her, pressing her to me, 'how you must have suffered!'

'Have you ever suffered anything similar, then?' she asked me. 'Are you like me? Have you often drenched your pillow in tears? Are the days of winter sunshine just as sad for you, too? When it is misty, in the evenings, and I am out walking by myself, it seems to me that the rain is falling through my heart and causing it to crumble into ruins.'

'But,' I replied, 'I doubt whether you have ever been as bored as I was in society – you had your days of pleasure, while for me it was as if I had been born in prison; there are countless things inside me that have never seen the light of day.'

'And yet you are so young! It's true: all men are old these days – children are as sated as old men, our mothers conceived us in a fit of boredom; people were different in olden times, weren't they?'

'Yes,' I replied, 'the houses we live in are all the same, white and mournful like the tombs in cemeteries; in the old black hovels that they're demolishing life must have been warmer; they sang their heads off, they smashed their tankards on the table, and they broke their bedsteads when they made love.'

'But who has made you so unhappy? You must have been in love?'

'Been in love?… My God, enough to envy your life!'

'Envy my life?' she said.

'Yes, envy it! After all, in your position I might have been happy, for if a man of the kind you desire doesn't exist anywhere, a woman of the kind I want must exist somewhere; among so many throbbing hearts there must be one for me.'

'Then look for it! Look for it!'

'Oh, have I ever been in love?… So much so that I am

saturated with repressed desires. No, you'll never know how many women have led me astray, whom in the depths of my heart I sheltered with an angelic love. Listen: when I had experienced a day in the company of a woman, I would say to myself, "If only I had known her for ten years! All those days of her life that I never even experienced in fact belonged to me; her first smile should have been for me, her first thought ever, for me. People come here and speak to her, she replies, she thinks about them... I should have read the books she admires. Why didn't I go out walking with her, beneath all the trees that sheltered her in their shade? There are so many dresses that she has worn out and that I never saw; in her life she has heard the most beautiful operas and I wasn't there; other men have already let her smell flowers that I did not pluck; I can't do anything about it, she will forget me, I am in her eyes just another passer-by in the street," And when I was separated from her, I would say to myself, "Where is she? What does she do, all day long, away from me? What does she spend her time in doing?" When a woman loves a man, she need only give him a signal, and he falls at her feet! But for us men, it's a matter of chance whether she even deigns to glance at us, and even then!... You have to be rich, possess horses to ride off on, own a house adorned with statues, give parties, throw money around, and make a noise; but as for living as one of the crowd, unable to dominate it by genius or wealth, and to remain thus as unknown as the most cowardly and stupid man of all, when you aspire to heavenly loves, when you would gladly die under the gaze of a beloved woman... that is a torment that I have known.'

'You're shy, aren't you? You're scared of women.'

'Not any more. Before, even the sound of their footsteps made me shudder, I would stand outside the hairdresser's shop gazing at the lovely wax heads with flowers and diamonds in their hair, all pink and white, with low-cut dresses; I fell in love with some of them. The display in a cobbler's shop would also keep me in raptures: in those little satin shoes, that were going to be taken away and worn at the evening ball, I would set a bare foot, a charming foot, with fine toenails, a foot of living alabaster, like that of a princess climbing into her bath; the corsets hanging outside fashion shops, and swaying in the wind, also filled me with bizarre longings; I offered bunches of flowers to women I didn't love, hoping that love would subsequently come along, as I had heard it might; I wrote letters addressed to someone quite insignificant, so that I could force myself to feel something by writing it down – and I wept; the least smile from a woman's mouth made my heart melt with delight, and then – nothing! So much happiness was not for me; who could ever love me?'

'Wait! Wait for one more year, for six months! Tomorrow perhaps – just keep hoping!'

'I have hoped too intensely ever to get what I hoped for.'

'You're talking like a child,' she told me.

'No, I cannot imagine there's even a love with which I would not be sated after twenty-four hours; I have dreamt of the feeling for so long that I am tired of it, like all those people one has cherished too intensely.'

'But it's the only beautiful thing in the world.'

'You're telling *me* that? I'd give anything to spend a single night with a woman who would love me.'

'Oh, if only, instead of hiding your heart away, you openly showed all the noble, kindly feelings that throb within it, every woman would be after you, they would all unfailingly strive to be your mistress; but you have been even crazier than me! Does anyone ever waste time over buried treasures? Only coquettes guess what people like you are really like, and they torture them: the others don't even see them. And yet you were well worth someone's love! Anyway, so much the better! I'm the one who will love you, I'm the one who will be your mistress.'

'My mistress?'

'Oh yes – please! I'll follow you wherever you want to go, I'll rent a room opposite yours, I'll gaze at you all the day long. I'll love you so much! To be with you, morning and evening, to sleep together at night, our arms wrapped round each other, to eat at the same table, facing one another, to get dressed in the same room, to go out together, and to feel you next to me! Aren't we made for one another? Don't your hopes go together with my bitter disillusionments? Your life and mine are just the same, aren't they? You'll tell me about all the trials and tribulations of your solitude, I will relate yet again the torments I have endured; we'll need to live as if we were only going to stay together for just one hour, exhaust all the pleasure and tenderness within us, and then begin all over again, and die together. Kiss me, kiss me again! Put your head just there on my breast, let me feel its weight, let your hair caress my neck, let my hands wander over your shoulders – you have such gentle eyes!'

The rumpled blanket, hanging to the ground, had left our feet bare; she rose to her knees and tucked it back under the mattress, and I saw her white back curving like a reed; our sleepless night had broken me; my forehead was heavy, my eyes so tired the eyelids smarted; she grazed them gently with a kiss, and this refreshed them as well as if they had been moistened with cold water. She too began to arouse herself more and more from the torpor into which she had for a moment subsided; aggravated by her fatigue, and inflamed by the savour of our previous caresses, she clasped me to her with desperate sensuality, telling me, 'Let's love one another, since nobody else has loved us – you are mine!'

She was panting, her mouth open, and kissing me with furious ardour; then, suddenly, she mastered her emotion, ran her hands through her ruffled hair, and added:

'Listen, how lovely our life would be if it could be like that, if we could go off to a land where yellow flowers grow in the sunshine and oranges ripen, on a shore – they do exist, apparently – where the sand is completely white, where the men wear turbans, and the women have dresses of gauze; we would lie at length under some great tree with its broad leaves, we would listen to the waves breaking on the curved shore, we would walk together by the side of the sea picking up seashells, I would weave baskets with reeds, and you would go off to sell them; I would dress you, I would curl your hair in my fingers, I'd place a necklace round your neck, oh! How I would love you! How I do love you! So let me drink my fill of you!'

Pinning me to her bed, with an impetuous movement, she flung her full length on my body and stretched her limbs out with an obscene, pale and quivering joy, her teeth clenched, and clutching me to her with a crazed strength; I felt as if I were being dragged into some hurricane of love, in which sobs and then piercing cries broke out; my lips, moist with her saliva, foamed and twitched; our muscles, locked into the same clench, clasped one another, knotted together as pleasure turned into delirium and ecstasy into torment.

Suddenly opening her eyes in a look of blank astonishment and alarm, she said:

'What if I were to have a child!'

And then, taking the contrary tack and becoming wheedling and imploring:

'Yes, yes, a child! A child from you!… You're leaving me?

We'll never see each other again, you'll never return, will you think of me sometimes? I'll always have a lock of your hair here: farewell!... Wait, it's hardly even daylight.'

So why was I in such a hurry to get away from her? Did I already love her?

Marie said nothing more to me, although I stayed with her a good half hour longer; she was perhaps thinking about her absent lover. There comes a moment, when we are separating, in which our sadness makes its presence felt in advance, and the beloved person is no longer with us.

We didn't say farewell; I took her hand, and she responded, but the strength she needed to grasp it had remained locked within her heart.

I never saw her again.

I have thought of her since, and not a day has gone by on which I have not wasted the greatest number of hours possible dreaming of her; sometimes I deliberately shut myself away, alone, and try to relive this memory; often I force myself to think about her before going to sleep, to dream of her at night – but that happiness has never been mine.

I sought her everywhere, out walking, at the theatre, at street corners, not knowing why I thought she would write to me; whenever I heard a carriage stop at my front door, I imagined she was about to get out. With what anguish did I follow certain women! With what a beating heart did I turn my head to see if it was her!

The house has been demolished, and no one has ever been able to tell me what became of her.

The desire for a woman one has obtained is something atrocious, a thousand times worse than the other desire: terrible images pursue you like a remorse. I am not jealous of the men who had her before me, but I *am* jealous of those who have had her since; a tacit convention had decreed, it seems to me, that we should remain faithful to one another; for over a year I remained faithful to that agreement, and then chance, boredom, and perhaps weariness with the same emotions led me to break it. But she was the one I pursued everywhere; in the beds of other women, I dreamt of her caresses.

However much one tries to sow new passions in the place where the old passions had grown, the old ones keep reappearing, and there is nothing in the world strong enough to tear them up by the root. Roman roads, along which the chariots of consuls used to roll, have long since fallen into disuse, and countless new tracks cut cross them; fields have risen over them, and corn now grows on them, but you can still see the trace they left, and their great stones can still inflict dents on farmers' ploughs.

The type of woman which almost all men seek is perhaps merely the memory of a love conceived in heaven, or in the first days of life; we seek everything even vaguely linked to it, and the second woman you fancy almost always resembles the first; you need a high degree of corruption or a very big heart to love absolutely everything. Look, too, at how it is always the same women who are spoken of by the men who write books – women that they describe a hundred times over without ever wearying. I knew a friend who had, at the age of fifteen, adored a young mother whom he had seen breastfeeding her child; for a long time he admired only women with nice plump figures; the beauty of slender women filled him with aversion.

As time went by, I loved her more and more; with the furious desire one has for impossible things, I concocted adventures that would enable me to find her again, and imagined our encounter; I recognised her eyes in the blue globules of rivers, and the colour of her face in the leaves of the aspen, when tinged with autumnal colours. Once, I was walking swiftly across a meadow, and the grass was swishing around my feet as I advanced; she was behind me. I turned round, there was no one there. Another day, a carriage passed in front of me, I looked up, a great white veil was dangling out of the window and fluttering in the wind, the wheels were turning, it twisted, called out to me, and disappeared; and I remained alone, distraught, more abandoned than if I had been at the bottom of a precipice.

Oh, if only we could extract everything there is inside us and create a person through the force of mere thought! If only we could grasp our phantom in our hands and touch its forehead, instead of wasting so many caresses and so many sighs on the empty air! Far from it: memory forgets and the image fades, while the pain persists grimly inside you. It was in order to remind myself of this fact that I have written the above, hoping that the words would enable me to relive it; I have failed; I know so much more than I have said.

In any case, it's a secret that I have told to no one – they'd have made fun of me. After all, they always mock those who love; it is a source of shame among men; everyone, either from modesty or egotism, hides away the best and most delicate of his soul's possessions; to gain the esteem of others, we must only ever show our ugliest sides; this is how we keep ourselves on the common level. 'You loved a woman like that?' they'd have said to me, and at first no one would have understood; so what would have been the point of opening my mouth?

They'd have been right; perhaps she was neither more beautiful nor more ardent than any other; I am afraid of loving something that is no more than a notion dreamt up by my mind, and of cherishing in her nothing other than the love of which she made me dream.

I struggled for a long time against this thought – that I had placed love on too high a pedestal to hope that it would come down to my level; but, from the persistence of this idea, I was forced to acknowledge that it was indeed something analogous. It was only a few months after leaving her that I felt it; to begin with, on the contrary, I lived in a state of great calm.

How empty the world is when you walk through it alone! What would I do in it? How would I spend my time? On what would I employ my intelligence? How long the days are! Where, then, is the man who complains of the brevity of the days of our life? Let them show him to me; he must be a happy mortal.

Take your mind off things, they say – but by doing what? They may as well say: try to be happy. How? And what's the use of all that agitation? Everything in nature is good: trees grow, rivers flow, birds sing, stars shine; but man in his torment twists and turns, rushes around, cuts down forests, overturns the earth, launches out to sea, travels, runs, kills animals, kills himself, perhaps, and weeps, and roars, and thinks about hell, as if God had given him a mind to conceive even more evils than those he endures!

In days gone by, before Marie, there was something fine and grand in my intense boredom; but now it is merely stupid – the boredom of a man sozzled with cheap brandy, asleep, dead drunk.

Those who have experienced a great deal are not the same. At the age of fifty, they are fresher than I was at twenty, and everything strikes them as still new and attractive. Will I be like those useless nags, who are tired no sooner than they are out of the stable, and who trot at ease only after they have gone a fair bit of the way, having at first limped painfully along? Too many sights make me feel ill, and too many others fill me with pity – or rather, they all merge into the same disgust.

The man who is well born and so doesn't want a mistress (since he couldn't lavish diamonds on her, or house her in a palace), and who witnesses vulgar love affairs, and calmly contemplates the imbecilic ugliness of those two rutting animals called a lover and his mistress, is not tempted to lower himself to their level; he wards off love as if it were a frailty, and he crushes beneath his knees all the desires that assail him; the struggle exhausts him. The cynical egotism of men makes me shun them, just as the narrow minds of women put me completely off their society; I am wrong, after all, since two lovely lips are worth more than all the eloquence in the world.

A fallen leaf flutters and flies off in the wind, and I too would like to fly away, far away, never to return, anywhere, so long as I could leave my own country; my home weighs me down, I have gone in and come out so often through the same door! I have raised my eyes so often to the same place, my bedroom ceiling – which ought by now to have been quite worn away by my gaze.

Oh, to feel yourself hunched on a camel's back! Before you there spreads a broad red sky, and expanses of uniform brown sand; a flaming horizon stretches away into the distance over the undulating terrain, and an eagle soars over your head; in one spot is a troop of storks with pink feet passing by on their way to the wells; the ship of the desert rocks you on its back, the sun makes you close your eyes and bathes you in its beams, you can hear nothing but the muffled tread of your mounts, the driver has just finished his song, on you go, on and on. In the evenings you push in the poles and pitch tent, you give the dromedaries a drink, you lie down on a lion skin, you have a smoke, you light fires to ward off the jackals you can hear yelping far away in the desert, unknown stars four times as big as ours twinkle in the sky; in the morning, you fill your water skins at the oasis, you set off again, all alone, the wind whistles, and the sand swirls up.

And then, in some plain through which you gallop all day long, palm trees rise between the columns and gently wave their foliage, next to the immobile shade of ruined temples; goats climb over the collapsed façades and nibble at the plants that have grown up among the embossed blocks of marble; they bound away when you draw near. Beyond that, after crossing forests in which the trees are woven together by gigantic creepers, and rivers whose other shores cannot be seen, lies the Sudan, the land of negroes, the land of gold; but even further, oh! let's keep going, I want to see fiery Malabar and its dances, which often end in death; the wines are as murderous as poisons, and the poisons as sweet as wines; the sea, a blue sea filled with coral and pearls, resounds to the tumult of the sacred orgies that take place in mountain caverns; you have left any haziness behind, the atmosphere here is crimson, the cloudless sky is mirrored in the warm ocean, the cables steam when you lift them out of the water, sharks follow after the ship and eat the dead.

Oh, India! India above all! White mountains, filled with pagodas and idols, in the middle of woods swarming with tigers and elephants, yellow men with white costumes, women the colour of tin with rings on their hands and feet, gauze dresses that swathe them like a vapour, and eyes of which all you can see are the lids blackened with henna; together they sing a hymn to some god, and dance... Dance, dance, dancing girl, daughter of the Ganges, let your feet spin in my head! Like a snake she bends backwards, lets her arms hang

85

loose, her head sways, her hips swing, her nostrils flare, her hair falls around her, the smoking incense rises up on every side of the stupid gilded idol with its four heads and twenty arms.

In a small boat of cedar wood – a long boat, whose slender oars resemble feathers – under a veil made of woven bamboo, to the sound of tam-tams and tambourines, I will go to the yellow country they call China; you can hold women's feet in your hands, their heads are small, and their eyebrows slender, and rise at the corners; they live in arbours of green reeds and eat velvet-skinned fruits off painted porcelain. A mandarin, with his pointed moustache falling down onto his chest, his head shaven, with a topknot that comes right down his back, and a round fan in his fingers, strolls through his gallery, where the tripods are burning, and places his feet slowly on the mats of rice; a little pipe is stuck through his pointed hat, and black Chinese characters are printed on his red silk clothes. Oh, how far I have travelled on the back of a tea chest!

Carry me away, tempests of the New World – you uproot age-old oaks and stir up the lakes where serpents frolic in the waves! May the mountain torrents of Norway cover me with their foam! May the snow of Siberia, which falls in thick dense heaps, cover my route! Oh, to travel, to travel, never stopping, and, in this immense waltz, to see everything appearing and vanishing away, until your skin cracks open and the blood spurts forth!

Let valleys follow mountains, fields follow cities, and plains follow seas. Let us go up and down the hillsides, let the spires of cathedrals disappear, as have the masts of the serried vessels in the harbours; let us listen to the cascades falling on the rocks, the winds sweeping through the forests, and the glaciers melting in the sunlight; let me see Arab horsemen galloping along, and women borne on palanquins; and then, domes arching and pyramids rising into the skies, stifling underground chambers where mummies slumber, narrow defiles where the brigand loads his weapon, rush-filled expanses in which the rattlesnake hides, striped zebras running through the tall grass, kangaroos perched on their hind legs, monkeys swaying from the branches of coconut trees, tigers pouncing on their prey, gazelles fleeing from them…

On, on! Let us sail over the wide oceans, where whales and cachalots are at war. Look: along comes, like some great sea bird beating its two wings, across the waves, the dugout canoe of the savages; bloody scalps hang from their prow, and they have painted their ribs red; their lips are split, their faces daubed, their noses pierced with rings, and they howl out their death chant; their green-tipped arrows are poisoned, so that you die in agony; their naked wives, with tattooed breasts and hands, raise great pyres for the victims of their menfolk, who have promised them white man's flesh that melts so nicely in the mouth.

Where shall I go? The earth is vast, I will follow every road to its end, I will empty every horizon, even though I perish while rounding the Cape, die of cholera in Calcutta, or of the plague in Constantinople!

If only I were a mule driver in Andalusia! Then I could trot along all day through the gorges of the sierras, watch the Guadalquivir flow by, on which there are islands of oleanders, hear, in the evenings, the guitars and the voices singing beneath the balconies, and watch the moon mirroring herself in the marble basin of the Alhambra, where once the wives of sultans would bathe.

I wish I were a gondolier in Venice or the driver of one of those carrioles which, in the fine season, take you from Nice to Rome! And yet there are people who actually live in Rome, people who need never leave. Happy the beggar in Naples who sleeps in broad daylight, asleep on the shore, and who, as he smokes his cigar, can also see the smoke from Vesuvius rising into the sky! I envy him his bed of pebbles and the dreams he can dream; the sea, unfailingly lovely, wafts to him the scent of its waves and the distant murmur that comes from Capri.

Sometimes I imagine arriving in Sicily, in a small village of fishermen, where all the boats have lateen sails. It's morning; there, between baskets and stretched-out nets, a working-class woman is sitting, barefoot; round her corset hangs a golden cord, as on the women of the Greek colonies; her black hair, separated into two tresses, falls down to her heels; she rises to her feet, and shakes out her apron; she walks along, and her figure is at once robust and supple, like that of an ancient nymph. If only I could be loved by such a woman! Some poor ignorant child, unable even to read – but her voice would be so sweet when she told me, in her Sicilian accent, 'I love you! Stay here!'

The manuscript stops here, but I knew its author, and if anyone has reached this page after making his way through all the metaphors, hyperboles and other figures that fill the previous pages, and now wishes to know how it ended, let him continue reading; we are about to tell him.

Feelings can be expressed in words only with great difficulty, otherwise this book would have been completed in the first person. Doubtless, our man must have concluded he had nothing else to say; there comes a point at which you stop writing and think all the more – it was at this point that he came to a halt: too bad for the reader!

I admire the way that chance so decided that the book should stop here, just when it could have been improved; the author was about to go out into society, he would have had countless things to teach us, but instead, he retired more and more into an austere solitude, from which nothing emerged. And he judged fit to stop complaining, perhaps because he began to suffer for real. Neither in his conversation, nor in his letters, nor in the papers I went through after his death, in which I found this narrative, did I ever come across anything that could disclose the state of his soul after the period at which he stopped writing his confessions.

His greatest regret was that he was not a painter; he said he had some really beautiful pictures in his imagination. He was also sorry not to be a musician; on spring mornings, when he would go for walks along the avenues of poplar trees, endless symphonies would echo through his head. In any case, he understood nothing of painting or music; I saw him admire real nonentities and come away from the Opera with a raging headache. With a little more time, patience, and hard work, and above all with a more sensitive taste for the formal aspect of the arts, he would have managed to write mediocre poetry, good enough for a lady's album – and this is always a gallant thing to do, whatever you may say.

In his earliest youth, he had drawn inspiration from really bad authors, as you may have seen from his style; as he grew older, he lost his taste for them, but the excellent authors just didn't fill him with the same enthusiasm.

He was a passionate devotee of beauty, and ugliness repelled him as much as crime; indeed, there is something quite dreadful about an ugly person; from a distance he fills you with horror, and from close up with disgust; when he speaks, you suffer; if he weeps, his tears irritate you; you feel like beating him up when he laughs and, in silence, his motionless face strikes you as the seat of every vice and every base instinct. So it was that he never forgave a man to whom he had taken a dislike at their very first encounter; on the other hand, he was perfectly devoted to people who had never spoken more than a few words to him, but whose way of walking or the cut of whose jib he liked.

He shunned gatherings, shows, balls and concerts, for hardly had he entered them than he felt himself filled with an icy gloom and his hair stood on end as if in a cold blast. When he was jostled by the crowd, a fresh new hatred rose to his heart, and he felt towards them all a wolfish hatred, that of a wild beast tracked down in his lair.

He had the vanity to believe that men did not like him – while men simply did not know him.

Public misfortunes and collective sorrows saddened him but little; I would even go so far as to say that he felt more pity for canaries in their cages, fluttering their wings when the sun shines, than for whole peoples condemned to slavery. This was just the way he was. He was full of delicate scruples and real sensitivity; for instance, he could not go into a tea room and see a poor man watching him eat without blushing to the ears; as he left, he would press all the money he had into his hand and flee. But he was considered cynical, because he called a spade a spade and said aloud what people usually keep to themselves.

The love of kept women (the ideal of young men who don't have the means to keep a woman themselves) was hateful to him, and filled him with disgust; he thought that the man who pays for his services is the master, the lord, the king. Although he was poor, he respected riches and not rich people; to be, for free and for nothing, the lover of a woman who is housed, dressed and fed by another man, struck him as about as witty as stealing a bottle of wine from another man's cellar; he would add that to boast of doing so was the characteristic of rascally servants and petty-minded men.

To want a married woman, and to make friends with her husband to this end, to shake his hand affectionately, to laugh at his puns, to sympathise with him when business was bad, to run errands for him, to read the same newspaper as him – in a word, to perform, in a single day, more base and vulgar actions than ten galley-slaves have done in their whole lives – was something too humiliating for his pride, and yet he did love several married women; sometimes he set out to woo them, but he would suddenly be seized by repugnance, when the lovely lady was already starting to simper at him, just as frosts in May nip apricot flowers in the bud.

And what about women of easy virtue, I hear you asking? Well, the answer is no! He couldn't bring himself to climb up into some garret to kiss a mouth that had just dined on cheese, and hold a hand covered with chilblains.

As for seducing a young woman, he would have felt less guilty if he had raped her; to yoke someone to you was for him worse than murdering her. He seriously thought that there is less harm in killing a man than producing a child: in the first case you are relieving someone of life, not his whole life, but a half or a quarter or a hundredth part of that existence that is going to finish, that would finish without you; but as for the second, he would say, are you not responsible to him for all the tears he will shed, from the cradle to the grave? Without you he would never have been born, and why *is* he born? For your amusement, not for his, that's for sure; to carry your name, the name of a fool, I'll be bound – you may as well write that name on some wall; why do you need a man to bear the burden of three or four letters?

To his eyes, the man who, basing his actions on the Civil Code, forcibly enters the bed of the virgin who has been given to him that same morning, thereby carrying out a legal rape that is protected by authority, had no counterpart among apes, hippopotami and toads; they at least, male and female, copulate when common desires lead them to seek out each other and unite, in such a way that there is neither terror and disgust on the one side, nor brutality and obscene despotism on the other; and he would set out long immoral theories to prove his point – though it would be futile to relate them here.

That is why he never married and took as his mistress neither a kept woman, nor a married woman, nor a woman of easy virtue, nor a girl; that left widows, and the thought of them didn't even cross his mind.

When he had to choose a profession, he hesitated between countless repellent possibilities. To be a philanthropist he wasn't cunning enough, and his kindly nature led him to shun medicine; as for commerce, he was incapable of calculating, and the mere sight of a bank set his nerves on edge. Despite his wild eccentricities, he had too much common sense to take seriously the noble profession of lawyer; in any case, his sense of justice would never have been able to fit in with existing laws. He had too much good taste to become a critic, and he was, perhaps, too much of a poet to succeed in literature. And anyway, are those really professions? *One needs to settle down in a good job and find a position in the world, one gets bored with idleness, one must make oneself useful, man is born to labour*: maxims that are difficult to grasp, though people took care to repeat them to him frequently.

Resigned to being bored everywhere and by everything, he declared he would study law, and he went to live in Paris. Many people in his village envied him his journey, and told him how lucky he was, able to hang out in cafés, take in shows, go to restaurants, and see beautiful women; he let them have their say, and he smiled in the same way one does when on the verge of tears. And yet, how often he had longed to leave his room once and for all, that room where he had yawned his head off, and where his elbows had worn out the mahogany surface of the old desk on which he had composed his dramas at the age of fifteen! And yet he found it hard to leave all that behind; it is, perhaps, the places that we have cursed most roundly that we prefer to the others – don't prisoners feel nostalgic for their prisons? The reason is that, in their prisons, they could still hope, whereas once they are out, they have nothing more to hope for; through the walls of their cells, they could see the countryside dotted with bright daisies, criss-crossed by streams, covered with yellow corn and tree-lined roads – but once they have been returned to liberty, to wretchedness, they again see life as it really is: a stony, bumpy road, muddy and icy, as is the countryside, so beautiful yet in reality thronged with local policemen who stop them picking fruit when they are thirsty, and appointed with forest rangers to prevent them killing game when they are hungry, and crawling with gendarmes if they feel like going out for a stroll and don't have their papers.

He took up lodgings in a furnished room, where the furniture had been bought for other lodgers, and worn threadbare by them; he thought he was living in ruins. He spent his days working, listening to the muffled noise from the street, and watching the rain falling onto the rooftops.

When it was sunny, he would go for a walk in the Luxembourg Gardens, scuffling through the fallen leaves, remembering how he had done just the same at school; but he had never suspected that, ten years later, he would still be doing exactly the same thing. Or else he would sit on a bench and think of countless sad and tender things, gazing at the cold, black water of the ponds, and returning home feeling sick at heart. Two or three times, not knowing what to do, he went into churches for the Benediction, and tried to pray; how much his friends would have laughed if they had seen him dipping his fingers into the holy water and making the sign of the cross!

One evening, as he was wandering round some streets and feeling so very angry, for no apparent reason, that he would have liked to throw himself against naked swords and fight to the death, he heard voices singing and the sweet sounds of an organ swelling and fading in reply. He went in. Beneath the portico, an old woman, squatting on the ground, was asking for alms as she rattled coppers in a tin-plate cup; the upholstered door swung to and fro every time someone went in or out; you could hear the clatter of clogs, and the scraping of chairs across the flags; at the far end, the chancel was lit, the tabernacle was gleaming amid the candles, the priest was chanting the prayers, the lamps, hanging in the nave, were swaying on their long chains, the tops of the ogive windows and the aisles were lost in shadow, the rain was beating on the stained-glass windows and rattling off their leads, the organ played on, and the voices resumed, as on the day when he had listened from the cliff tops as the sea and the birds spoke to each other. He was filled with the desire to be a priest, so he could say prayers over the bodies of the dead, wear a hair shirt and prostrate himself, overwhelmed by the love of God... Suddenly a guffaw of pity rose from the depths of his heart; he pulled his hat firmly down over his ears, and left with a shrug.

More than ever he fell into a sadness, more than ever the days seemed long to him; the barrel organ that he could hear playing under his window tugged at his heartstrings; he found that these instruments had an irresistible melancholy, and he would say that those musical boxes were full of tears. Or rather, he didn't say anything at all, since he didn't try to pass himself off as bored and blasé, as the man who is disillusioned by everything; eventually, indeed, people found he had become more cheerful in character. It was, more often than not, some poor man from the south of France, or from Piedmont or Genoa, who was turning the handle on the barrel-organ. Why had such a man left his mountain home, and his hut crowned with maize at harvest? He would watch him for a long time, with his big square head, his black beard and his suntanned hands, a little monkey dressed in red hopping around on his shoulder pulling faces; the musician would hold out his cap, and he flung a few coins down into it, and followed him until he was out of sight.

Opposite him, a house was being built; it took three months. He saw the walls rising, the storeys mounting one on top of another; the panes were fitted into the windows, it was whitewashed and painted, and then the doors were closed; households moved in and started to live their lives there; he was annoyed to have neighbours, he would have preferred the sight of stones.

He would saunter through museums, gazing at all those painted, motionless portraits, forever young in their ideal lives – all those portraits of famous people one goes to see, and who watch the crowds go by without lifting their hands from their swords: their eyes will still be shining when our grandsons are dead and buried. He would lose himself in the contemplation of ancient statues, especially those that were mutilated.

There was one rather sad event that occurred: one day, in the street, he thought he recognised someone passing close by him; the stranger, likewise, had given a start; they halted in their tracks and went up to one another. It was him! His old friend, his best friend, his brother, the boy he had always had by his side at school, in class, at private study, in the dormitory; they did their impositions and their homework together; in the schoolyard and when they went out for walks, they would always stroll along arm in arm; they had sworn in bygone days to live together, sharing everything, and to remain *friends till death did them part*. First they shook hands, calling each other by name, then they looked each other up and down from head to toe in silence – both of them had changed and aged somewhat already. After asking each other what they now did, they stopped and didn't know how to continue; they had not seen each other for six years and they couldn't think of anything else to say. Finally bored and irritated at gazing straight into one another's eyes, they separated.

As he had no energy for anything, and as time, despite what the philosophers have said about it, seemed to him the form of wealth least capable of being borrowed, he started to drink brandy and to smoke opium; he would frequently spend his days lying flat on his back, half drunk, in a state midway between apathy and nightmare.

At other times his strength would return to him, and he would suddenly bounce back like a coiled spring. Then, work appeared to tempt him again, and the glowing radiance of thought brought a smile to his lips, the serene and profound smile of the wise; he quickly settled down to work, he had superb plans, he wanted to show certain periods in a completely new light, to link art with history, to interpret the great poets as well as the great painters, and with this aim in view he would need to learn languages, to go back to Antiquity and to become acquainted with the Orient; he could see himself already reading inscriptions and deciphering obelisks; then he decided he was crazy, and folded his arms again.

He had stopped reading, or rather he read books that he thought were bad and that nonetheless gave him a certain pleasure through their very mediocrity. At night he could not sleep, he twisted and turned sleeplessly on his bed, he dozed and dreamt and woke up again, with the result that, when morning came, he was more tired than if he had stayed awake all night.

Worn out by the terrible habit of boredom, and even deriving a certain pleasure from the mindless state that results, he was like those people who watch themselves die; he didn't open his window to get a breath of fresh air, he no longer bothered to wash his hands, he lived in the squalor of poverty, wearing the same shirt for a whole week; he stopped shaving and combing his hair. Although he felt the cold, if he had gone out in the morning and got his feet wet, he would keep the same shoes on all day without lighting a fire, or else he would throw himself fully clothed onto his bed and try to get off to sleep; he watched the flies running across the ceiling, he smoked and followed with his eyes the little blue spirals that coiled upwards from his lips.

The reader will easily realise that he had no aim in life, and that was precisely the nub of his problem. What could have spurred him on and inspired him? Love? He shunned it; ambition made him laugh; as for money, he was thoroughly rapacious, but his sloth got the upper hand, and then a million francs wasn't worth the trouble of gaining it, in his view; luxury befits a man born in opulence; the man who has actually earned his fortune almost never knows what to do with it; and his pride was so great that he would have turned down a throne. You will ask me, 'What did he want?'

I don't know, but one thing is for sure: he had no intention of getting himself elected to parliament later on; he would even have refused a post as prefect, including the embroidered uniform, the cross of the Legion of Honour around his neck, and the buckskins and riding boots worn on ceremonial occasions. He preferred to read André Chénier than to be a minister, and he would rather have been Talma than Napoleon.[5]

He was a man who inclined to pretentiousness and rambling speeches, in which he indulged in an excessive use of epithets.

Surveyed from these heights, the earth vanishes, as do all the prizes for which people struggle on its surface. There are also sufferings from the heights of which a person seems to be nothing and yet despises everything else; when these sufferings don't kill you, suicide alone can deliver you from them. He did not kill himself, but went on living.

Carnival time came; he took no pleasure in it. He did everything at the wrong time; funerals almost aroused his merriment, and the theatre made him feel gloomy; he kept imagining that there was a throng of elegantly attired skeletons, with their gloves, their muffs, and their feather hats, leaning out of their boxes, gazing at each other through their opera glasses, putting on airs and graces, and staring at each other with empty eyes; in the pit he saw, gleaming under the light of the candelabras, a throng of white skulls packed closely together. He heard men rush down the stairs, laughing; they were going off with women.

A memory from his youth flashed through his head; he thought of X***, that village to which he had one day walked, and which he himself describes in what you have just read; he wished to see it again before he died, as he felt his strength ebbing. He put money in his pocket, picked up his coat and set off straight away. The last days of carnival, that year, had fallen at the start of February; it was still very chilly, the roads were frozen, the carriage bowled along; he sat in the coupé, not sleeping, but enjoying the sensation of being swept along to that sea that he would gaze on again; he watched the postilion's reins, lit up by the lantern on the roof, as they swayed in the air and flicked on the steaming cruppers of the horses; the sky was pure and the stars were shining as on the finest summer nights.

Around ten o'clock in the morning, he got off at Y*** and from there made his way on foot to X***; he walked quickly, this time – indeed, he ran along to keep warm. The ditches were filled with ice, the trees, still bare, were red at the tips of their branches, the fallen leaves, that had rotted in the rain, formed a great black and steel-grey layer, which covered the foot of the forest trees. The sky was a hazy white, and sunless. He noticed that the road signs had been overturned; at one place they had been felling wood since he had last passed that way. He hurried along, in haste to arrive. Finally the terrain started to slope downwards; at this point he took a familiar path across the fields, and soon he saw, in the distance, the sea. He stopped; he could hear it beating against the shore and roaring on the horizon, *in altum*; he could smell a salty tang, wafted to him on the cold winter breeze; his heart beat faster.

A new house had been built at the entrance to the village, and two or three others had been demolished.

The boats were out at sea, the quay was deserted, everyone was staying at home; long icicles, which the children call *the kings' candles*, were hanging from the eaves and gutters, the shop signs of the grocer and the tavern-keeper creaked and groaned on their iron supports, the sea was rising and sweeping in over the pebbles, with a noise of chains and sobs.

After he had breakfasted (and he was surprised not to be hungry), he went for a walk along the beach. The wind was singing through the air, the slender rushes growing in the dunes were whistling as they furiously tossed and swayed, flecks of foam flew from the shore and blew in over the sand, and sometimes a gust of wind would carry them up into the clouds.

Night came – or rather, that long twilight that precedes it on the gloomiest days of the year; thick snowflakes fell from the sky and melted into the waves, but they lingered for a long time on the beach, spattering it with great silver tears.

He saw, in one place, an old boat half buried in the sand; it might have foundered there twenty years previously. Sea fennel had grown in it, and polyps and mussels clung to its green, decaying planks; he loved this boat, and walked right round it, touching it in different places, and gazed at it with a singular intensity, the way one gazes at a corpse.

A hundred paces further on, there was a little place in the hollow of a rock, where he had often gone to sit and spend hour after wonderful hour doing nothing – he would take a book and not read it, he would settle down there all by himself, lying on his back, to gaze at the blue of the sky between the white walls of the vertical rocks; it was here that he had dreamed his sweetest dreams, it was here that he had most enjoyed listening to the mew of the gulls, and the sea wrack had dangled down and shaken over him the pearls of its hair; it was here that he saw the ships' sails dip beneath the horizon, and the sun, for him, had been warmer here than in any other place on earth.

He went back and there it was; but others had taken

possession of it, since, as he mechanically rooted around in the ground with his foot, he unearthed a broken bottle and a knife. People had had a party here, no doubt; they'd come here with ladies, they'd had a picnic, they'd been laughing and joking. 'Oh God,' he said to himself, 'isn't there anywhere on earth that we have loved enough, and where we have lived enough, for it to belong to us until we die, and that nobody else can ever set eye on?'

So he made his way back up the ravine, where he had so often kicked the stones down; sometimes indeed he had deliberately flung them down, to hear them bash against the walls of the rocks and rouse a solitary echo in response. On the plateau overlooking the cliff, the air became sharper, he saw the moon rising opposite, in a patch of blue, dark sky; under the moon, on the left, there was a little star.

He was weeping – was it from cold or sadness? His heart was bursting, he needed to talk to someone. He went into a tavern, where he had sometimes gone for a beer, and asked for a cigar; he could not refrain from saying to the young woman serving him, 'I've been here before'. She replied, 'Oh! but it's not in season now, m'sieu, it's not in season,' and she gave him his change.

That evening he wanted to go out again; he went to lie in a hollow used by hunters to shoot wild ducks. He saw for a moment the image of the moon floating up and down on the waves and twisting on the sea's surface, like a great serpent; then on every side of the sky, the clouds piled up again, and everything went black. In the darkness, dim waves rose and fell, overtaking one another and booming like a hundred cannon; a sort of rhythm turned this noise into a terrible melody, and the shore, shaking under the crash of the waves, replied to the echoing full tide.

He reflected for a moment whether it wouldn't be better to make an end of it; no one would see him, there would be no one to rescue him, in three minutes he would be dead. But then, thanks to a complete change-around that is common at such moments, life seemed to smile on him again, his existence in Paris struck him as attractive, with a great future ahead; he saw his good old work room, and all the tranquil days he would still be able to spend there. And yet, the voices of the abyss were calling to him, the waves were opening like a grave, ready to close over him at once and envelop him in their liquid folds...

He felt afraid and went back to his lodgings; all night long he heard the wind whistling, and it filled him with terror; he lit a huge fire and warmed himself up, positively roasting his legs.

He had reached his journey's end. Back home, he found his windows white with hoar frost, in the fireplace the coal had gone out, his clothes were still on the bed just where he had left them, the ink had dried in the inkwell, and the walls were cold and dripping.

He said to himself, 'Why didn't I stay back there?' and he thought bitterly of the joy with which he had set out.

Summer returned, and it made him no happier. Sometimes, however, he would go out to the Pont des Arts, and watch the trees in the Tuileries swaying, and the rays of the setting sun lighting the sky crimson, passing through the Arc de Triomphe as through a rainbow.

Finally, last December, he died, but slowly, little by little, by mere dint of thinking, without any organ being affected, the way one dies of sadness – which will appear rather difficult to people who have suffered a great deal; but you have to put up with it in a novel, for love of the marvellous.

He recommended that they carry out an autopsy as he was afraid of being buried alive; but he strictly forbade them to embalm him.

– 25th October 1842

NOTES

1. Michel Eyquem de Montaigne (1533–92) was one of Flaubert's favourite authors. This quotation is from the *Essays*, book II, chapter 3, where Montaigne writes, 'If to philosophise is to doubt, as they say, then to indulge in foolery and fantastication – as I do – must be an even better way of doubting.'

2. René was the hero of Chateaubriand's story of the same name (first published separately in 1805). A gloomy young man who ended his days among the Indians of North America, René epitomised romantic world-weariness; Werther, the hero of Goethe's *The Sorrows of Young Werther* (1774), suffered from unrequited love and committed suicide.

3. A reference to the Juggernaut, the image of the god Krishna that was carried on an enormous cart under whose wheels his devotees are said to have thrown themselves.

4. *Paul et Virginie* (one of Emma Bovary's favourite novels), by Bernardin de Saint-Pierre (1737–1814), was first published separately in 1789; it is set on an idyllically described island of Mauritius, and Paul and Virginie, who are brought up there together almost as brother and sister, fall in love. *Les crimes des reines de France depuis le commencement de la monarchie jusqu'à Marie-Antoinette*, was published anonymously in 1791 and details the crimes of queens: Messalina (17–48) was the debauched wife of the Roman emperor Claudius; Theodora (*c.*500–48) the lascivious consort of the Byzantine emperor Justinian; Marguerite of Burgundy (1290–1315) the allegedly adulterous wife of King Louis, who had her strangled; Mary Stuart (1542–87) the somewhat fickle Queen of Scots, who may have connived in the murder of her husband Lord Darnley; and Catherine II (the Great) (1729–96), Empress of Russia and also rather free with her favours. The two works are presumably being used by Flaubert to foreground the themes of feminine innocence (Virginie is so modest that she drowns at sea, refusing to allow a sailor to carry her to shore since it will mean taking off her clothes) versus feminine experience.

5. André Chénier (1762–94), often considered the best French poet of the eighteenth century, was guillotined during the Terror. François-Joseph Talma (1763–1826) was a great tragic actor admired by, among others, Napoleon.

BIOGRAPHICAL NOTE

Gustave Flaubert was born in Rouen in 1821, the son of a renowned surgeon and physician. In early life Flaubert demonstrated a love for history and literature, and went on to study law in Paris, where, among others, he made the acquaintance of the writer Victor Hugo. A subsequent attack of epilepsy caused Flaubert to abandon his legal studies, but this change of direction was to give him the freedom and solace he desired to concentrate on his writing, over which he laboured painstakingly, and for which he even broke off his much-celebrated love affair with Louise Colet. Following his father's death in 1846, Flaubert lived in Croisset, occasionally travelling to exotic locations such as Egypt, Turkey, and also Tunisia, where he undertook research for his richly detailed novel, *Salammbô*.

His first published novel, *Madame Bovary*, appeared in 1857, having taken him five years to write. It immediately provoked a public outcry for its seeming lack of morality. Despite this reaction, Flaubert found himself increasingly respected and admired in artistic circles, and was a regular guest at literary gatherings in Paris. He went on to pen a number of highly acclaimed works – including *Sentimental Education*, his most ambitious work, published in 1869, and *Three Tales*, published in 1877. It is both for his novels and for his remarkable correspondence (detailing his ideas on the life of the artist and the act of writing) that he has been hailed as a true master of nineteenth-century fiction. Flaubert died in 1880.

Andrew Brown studied at the University of Cambridge, where he taught French for many years. He now works as a freelance teacher and translator. He is the author of *Roland Barthes: the Figures of Writing* (OUP, 1993), and his translations include *Memoirs of a Madman* by Gustave Flaubert, *For a Night of Love* by Emile Zola, *The Jinx* by Théophile Gautier, *Mademoiselle de Scudéri* by E.T.A. Hoffmann, *Theseus* by André Gide, *Incest* by Marquis de Sade, *The Ghost-seer* by Friedrich von Schiller, *Colonel Chabert* by Honoré de Balzac, *Memoirs of an Egotist* by Stendhal, *Butterball* by Guy de Maupassant and *With the Flow* by Joris-Karl Huysmans, all published by Hesperus Press.